A SMALL TOWN SPRING

A ROSEDALE NOVEL

ELLE WATERS

ALSO BY ELLE WATERS

His Birthday Wish

His Christmas Love Song

His Fake Wedding Date

New Beginnings

Day Dreaming

His Ever After Collection

Rosedale

His Coffee Shop Crush

Rosedale Seasons

Cool for the Summer

Autumn Crush

Winter Under the Covers

A Small Town Spring

For Amanda

SPRING

KINGSTON

<h1 style="text-align:center">ONE</h1>

IT'S spring at last and I am ready to spring out of the city for a weekend in the country.

I whistle to myself as I step into the mirror-lined elevator and hit the button for the garage nine floors below. I'm escaping the city as early as possible this fine Friday morning. There's a little work in my LV shoulder bag, but mostly I'm going to Rosedale to unplug.

In the garage, I greet Mason the weekday garage attendant with a grin, which I temper when I remember his asthmatic grandson was in the hospital with bronchitis a few days ago.

"How's Jaden?" I ask as he gets my key from the box.

"Doing much better," he says. "They gave him a new inhaler, and it's working."

"Great news." I take the key from his outstretched hand and walk to a nearby bay. I pay extra to keep my baby close enough to extract it myself. "Have a good weekend."

"You too, Mr. James." Mason's old school—won't call me Kingston no matter how many times I ask. It's a remnant of old-style Manhattan manners I confess to taking pleasure in. It may be why I chose this building, Central Park-adjacent, complete with doorman and snooty neighbors. I myself am one of the snooty neighbors, even if my one-bed one-bath is one of the smallest apartments. Size, in this case, doesn't matter. It's a place to live during the week while I'm working at the Fenster Literary Agency, where I have sixteen children's and young adult authors on my list and bring in more revenue than the next three best-performing agents combined. But it's not home.

Home is where I'm headed once I stash my bag in the trunk of my gleaming San Remo Green BMW 8 Series. I've had the convertible for six months, but this might be the first day I'll actually be able to put the top down on my drive to Connecticut. On a good day, it takes two hours door to door. Fingers crossed traffic will cooperate today. I've got a podcast loaded up, a green tea latte in my Ember travel mug. I'm ready to go.

I cut across the park and hook up with the Henry Hudson, my foot on the pedal nice and heavy as I accelerate for all of twenty seconds before I'm forced to brake for the inevitable logjam. I sigh. It's the worst part of my bifurcated living situation. I could take the train, but it takes almost as long, and I need a car to get around Rosedale.

My podcast is interrupted by a voice alert that I have a text. I poke a button and a sonorous male British accent floods my car. It's the voice I've chosen for my phone's virtual assistant, who I jokingly call Jarvis. Jarvis reads out a text from Pete Blekitny.

"Dinner tonight at ours? Having a couple people over I want you to meet."

I never say no to dinner with two of my favorite people. I'd love Pete and his husband, Jack Avery, even if they weren't my highest-earning clients.

But I can't make it too easy on them. I poke another button and Jarvis takes a memo for me. "Depends. What are we having?"

The return message comes as the Henry Hudson gives way to the Cross County. "Donovan and Beck are coming too, and they're in charge of the menu."

Beck is almost as good a cook as he is a baker, and even if he's ordering food, he won't put out anything less than a top-tier spread. "I'm in. Who are the mysterious guests?"

Instead of a text, I get a phone call. "I know you're driving," Pete says, his warm voice competing with traffic noise, even as slow as I'm going.

"Feels more like I'm parked on the parkway, but so it goes." I sigh. "So, who do you want me to meet? Is this a ploy to set me up with one of Jack's rich, handsome Texan cousins?"

"Nope, not a set-up. I'm wooing a local artist to join the Art Center board, so I need you to charm her."

"I charm everyone," I say, inching the car forward a few feet. The V8 engine growls with restraint.

"Yes, you do," Pete agrees. "So come be your charming self."

"What can I bring?"

"Just you."

"I actually wanted to talk to you and Jack about something this weekend, so if there's no opportunity tonight, maybe we can plan something for later on?"

"Sure—Cleo, stop—uh, gotta go. Cleo's decided Daddy's slipper is her new chew toy."

"Which Daddy?" I ask.

"Jack," he says, sounding distracted. "See you tonight."

"Ciao," I get in before he ends the call. I chuckle and flip back to my podcast. It's a book podcaster interviewing an agent named Stephanie Collier. I've never met her, but she represents a lot of successful commercial fiction authors. I heard through the agent grapevine she's not happy at her agency.

Leaving Fenster to set up under my own shingle is something I've been thinking about for a while. If I could get someone as established as Stephanie to join forces with me, it would send a clear signal to the publishing world that I'm here for the long haul, that I'm someone who wants to leave a legacy. I believe I could make a difference. Agents often have the least security in the publishing food chain. What if I could nurture new agents by offering them health insurance and other benefits while they're waiting to land their first deals?

It's not impossible, and I need a new challenge. I'm financially secure, can buy anything I want, within reason. I paid off my mom's mortgage, helped my sister and her husband move back to Atlanta so someone's there to make sure Mom goes to her doctor's appointments after her heart attack a few years ago. I'm killing it both at work and in life, with friends who truly care about me.

The only thing I don't have is someone riding in the passenger seat of my precious Beamer. No one to curl up next to in bed as I work through my infinite to-be-read pile. No one to be my plus-one to dinner tonight, where I'll be surrounded by adorable unavailable gay men who've already found their forever person.

I never used to care about that stuff—finding The One, the person who I'd joyfully sign up to be with for the rest of my life. I had fun in my twenties—New York City was a revelation after spending my childhood in the Atlanta suburbs. I slowed down some in my thirties—I got choosier about who I brought home once I bought my apartment. Too many guys saw my address and assumed I'd be up for some kind of sugar daddy arrangement. I'm not against being the bigger breadwinner, but I'm old-fashioned—I find a work ethic attractive.

And then I met Sergio, and I thought, well, this is close. He was attractive, smart, kind, and successful in his own right. He even had a dog. And we got along like we'd known each other all our lives. He was almost like... a brother. The sex tapered off, but we gelled in so many other ways, it didn't seem to matter. But when he got the chance to take on a project in Seattle, it didn't hurt as much as I'd thought it would to say goodbye. It felt as if we were returning to the relationship we always should have had—as good friends.

He'll always be in my life, always be my friend. But since we stopped seeing each other, I've sort of given up on the idea of casual dating. I'm too old. It takes too much effort. And if I could be content with work and my shiny objects, with being able to jet off to Paris for a long weekend whenever I want or buy a new painting for my living room without checking with anyone else first, then I'd be golden.

But there's a part of me that wants what my friends have. If only I could skip dating and wake up next to a handsome husband one day.

I know that's not how relationships happen. I've helped my friends through their own romantic problems enough times to know that it takes work, it takes being vulnerable—it takes courage to end up with the person who's going to be the perfect fit to ride around in my passenger seat.

So until a miracle happens, I'll have to be content with driving solo.

The traffic ahead of me opens up and I hit the gas.

MY COTTAGE IS JUST as I left it when I was last here. I'm in Rosedale about two weekends a month, sometimes more if I can arrange to work from home for a few days. I carefully ease my car onto the gravel driveway, then maneuver it onto the concrete slab next to the house. I kill the engine, imagining how fantastic it will be to one day pull into the same space, only for it to be a real garage. The previous owners poured the slab to build a freestanding one-car garage, but never finished the project. It's been pretty low on my priority list given the amount of time I'm here, but I'd love to have covered parking for my beloved Beamer. Someday.

I unlock the front door. The scents of wood, honey,

and lemon greet me. It's not a huge house, but it serves me better than fine. There's a guest room and bath, a small living room dominated by a green velvet armchair whose twin lives in my bedroom. A counter-height bar separates the good-sized kitchen from a modest dining area. The big bedroom suite in the back has doors to the back patio, where I keep a grill and table and chairs. Outdoor dining is doable six months of the year. It's not quite warm enough for breakfast out there but give it another month.

I drop my bag and go straight to the wine fridge. Pete told me not to bring anything to dinner, but I don't like showing up empty-handed. I pick out a rosé, optimistic that it will work with whatever Beck has in store for us.

My phone rattles with a notification from my sister, Lucetta. It's a picture of my nephews, twin six-year-olds, their brown curls dusted in flour and their faces mottled by random purple splotches. Three words—*making blueberry pancakes*—are all the context I need. I grin, wishing someone could invent a teleportation device so I could pop down to Atlanta whenever I need a dose of nephew love.

A snazzy teleportation device would make traveling back and forth from the city easier, too. I crack my back, stiff after my extra-long car trip. It seems half the folks in Manhattan decided in unison to escape the city on this fine spring weekend.

By the time I check my email and message my assistant to make sure nothing urgent has come up, it's nearly time to head to Jack and Pete's. If Pete needs me to be charming, my threads might need an upgrade. I fell in love with this house at first sight when I was looking for a weekend hideaway from the city, but what really sold me was the bedroom suite's closet. Do not underestimate the importance of a well-designed closet. Mine is a walk-in I've outfitted with recessed lighting, a floor-to-ceiling mirror, and everything from shoe cubbies to shallow drawers for my watches and cuff link collection. There's an entire corner devoted only to ties. It's a very Carrie Bradshaw closet, which I say with all due respect.

My love of paisley has become so well known that it's now a bit of a cliché, and I find myself opting for different patterns lately. It's good to have a signature—fedoras are also my tried-and-true—but tonight I feel like mixing it up. I keep my fine camel-colored wool trousers, tailored to perfection, exchange my plain white dress shirt for a lavender one in a nod to the changing season. A darker purple necktie is next, then—what the hell, I throw on a pair of purple spats. They're snazzy and if I can't splash out with my friends, when can I? I grab my current favorite blazer—a brown velvet number that still works despite the slightly warming air. It's Connecticut in April, not the Caribbean. I leave my hair unadorned—I visited the barber yesterday and my locs are tidy. The longest ones brush my shoulders, but I gather them up in a thick handful and pull them away from my face with a sturdy black elastic.

I squint at the image gazing back at me, checking for wrinkles or any hint of gray in my hair. I touch my neck— is there an extra line that wasn't there yesterday? Most days I'd say I look younger than my thirty-seven years. But suddenly I feel old and tired. I've pushed myself my entire life to get here. It was exhausting, if rewarding. It paid off.

I just didn't anticipate ending up having to enjoy the fruits of my labors all by my lonesome.

Enough with the melancholy. I check my watch, grab my keys. The Beamer starts up with the push of a button, sounding sweet as a purring kitten. It's a pity Jack and Pete live a mere half mile away. In warmer weather, I'd walk, but on this bright spring day, I drive.

TWO

A COUPLE of Jack and Pete's guests have arrived ahead of me, and it seems they've put them to work already, because it's not tall, golden Pete who answers the door, or his husband, almost-as-tall, green-eyed Jack, but Donovan Eastman, known as Van to his friends, and Donovan to his besotted boyfriend, Beck Avery, Jack's cousin.

Van's got screen-star good looks, which makes sense because he's an actor, mainly theater, but some commercials and TV spots. He and I hooked up ages ago, but now we're more like brothers, held together by the glue that is Jack and Pete and their determination to bring all of their friends into the Rosedale lifestyle, such as it is. Van's still got one foot in the city, like me, but he and Beck are renovating a house together a couple of streets away, and he seems perfectly happy to be in his small-town-domestic-bliss era.

I guess when you find the right person, committing to something that huge makes sense.

Van greets me with a pat on the shoulder and brings

me through the light, airy house and into the big white kitchen with dark blue accents. Beck's at the stove, stirring a pot of something that smells like onions and heaven. Without pausing, he grabs a nearby open bottle of white wine and throws in an enormous glug.

"Kingston!" The way Beck's face lights up at my entrance might make a guy feel special, except that's how he is with everyone, even the strangers who come into his cookie shop on Main Street. He's a fountain of youthful energy and positivity.

I walk around the big kitchen island to give him a buss on the cheek, peer into the pot. "Risotto. How did you know that's exactly what I've been craving?"

"It was Donovan's idea, and now I'm worried it's going to be too dry." Fretting, Beck reaches for the wine again.

"I'm sure it'll be creamy as sin," I say, taking the bottle out of his hands and examining the label. I whistle when I recognize the vintage. "If this is what you're using for the risotto, what are we drinking tonight? I brought a rosé, but nothing on this level."

"Ask Pete. He picked out the wine," Van says. "He really wants to impress the guests of honor. He and Jack are upstairs getting dressed."

"I better check his work," I say. My friends, decked out as their kitchen is, don't have a wine fridge, so I head to the regular one while making a mental note for this year's Christmas present. Luckily, there are several bottles of nice bubbly already chilling. Unless their guests don't like hundred-dollar bottles of champagne, Pete can't go wrong. I see some decent reds on the counter, too. My boy's got this.

"Tell me what's happening, Van. Haven't seen you in a while." I crack the bottle of rosé for an aperitif and pour myself a glass. "Want some?"

Van shakes his head and holds up his beer. "I was in the city last week, but didn't have time to get in touch."

"New play?"

"Auditions, mostly," he says. "But I booked a guest spot on some crime show that shoots in a couple of weeks. And we decided what we're doing for Shakespeare in the Park at the Art Center this summer."

"You're in on that?"

He smiles sheepishly. The man who used to pooh-pooh local theater has become a vocal proponent of the Rosedale Art Center's theater department. "I'm co-directing with Dulcie. My first directing credit."

I thump him on the back. "All right. I'll have to clear my schedule to catch opening night. What are you performing?"

"We're going to do *Much Ado About Nothing*."

"One of my favorites. Can't wait to see what you and Dulcie do with it."

"Thanks, Kingston."

"And how is the cookie business, Beckett?"

Van wrinkles his nose at my use of Beck's full name. I smirk inwardly. I do it because I'm a literary snob and I enjoy the allusion. And it's fun to see Van, who used to chase tail like it was his job, get jealous over a simple familiarity. If I don't have anyone to get jealous over, might as well have some fun with my friends. Besides, Beck is completely devoted to his man.

"The shop is about to celebrate its seven-month

anniversary," Beck says, turning the flame off under the risotto. "And I hired a couple of new people for up front."

"Nice. How's your house?"

"It's a wreck," Beck says happily, "but we're almost done with the kitchen."

"We found mold in the basement," Van says dryly. "So remediating that is going to be a bitch. But remodeling is a marathon, not a sprint."

"You're doing a great job with the place."

"So now you've caught up on us, what about you?" Van asks.

"Same old," I say, shrugging. I don't mention my business idea because I want to run it by Jack before I let it out into the wider world. "I had a client debut at the top of the list last week, so that was pretty cool." Not the first time, but it's always amazing to be able to make that call.

"Congrats," Van says. "You seeing anybody?"

The question takes me by surprise, and I stumble over my response. "I—why do you ask?"

"There's a guy I know who recently moved to the city. Thought you two might want to hang out," Van says offhandedly.

I feel my eyebrows touch in the middle with how hard I'm staring him down. "You're trying to set me up?" That's a first.

Van's tan cheeks get a shade darker. "Look, if you aren't interested, no harm. He's a good guy, though."

"Attractive?" I ask, still suspicious. I remember Van's threat to me when I meddled in, scratch that, *aided out of the kindness of my heart,* his and Beck's budding romance.

He swore he'd retaliate one day when I fell in love. Maybe this is his way of paying me back.

"He's good-looking," Van says evasively. "He's an actor —or trying to be. I think he's temping right now."

"Sounds young. You know I'm not really into the Daddy thing." I touch my tie self-consciously.

"He's mid-twenties."

"And you don't look a day over thirty," Beck adds with the overconfidence of a twenty-six-year-old.

"Thanks," I say flatly. To Van, I say, "But no thanks."

"You're not dating?" Van asks, sounding surprised.

"I'm—" Again, the question stops me. I struggle to remember the last date I was on. The last guy I hooked up with. There have been men since Sergio, but they've been few and far between. I guess I've lost my taste for the casual, and the serious is—well, I haven't met anyone I want to be serious about.

I'm saved from having to explain myself to my annoyingly well-meaning friends by our hosts coming into the kitchen. Jack's laughing quietly while Pete's got his hand at the small of Jack's back. Cleo, their brown rescue mutt, twines around their feet before coming to greet me by sniffing at my purple shoes. I pat her head, then go to the sink to wash my hands.

Turning away from the happy couples gives me a chance to collect myself. I'm surprised to feel this unsettled by Van's simple offer of an introduction, and the fact that I'm older than everyone in this room, and I'm also the only single one.

How, exactly, did this happen?

My singleness was supposed to be a phase. For years, I

embraced dating, hookups, experimentation, infatuation, heartbreak, embarrassment, getting hurt, accidentally hurting others. I've had significant relationships—some even lasted a year or two, like Sergio. I've been through it all. But singledom has stubbornly stuck to me like a burr in my favorite camel hair coat—unable to be removed unless I cut it out and ruin the coat forever.

But it's not their fault—my paired-off friends haven't done anything wrong. In fact, I urged them together, at least in Van and Beck's case. It's sweet, I guess, that Van wants to return the favor. But if I know anything at all, it's that love doesn't work like that. It doesn't work on a planned-out schedule or just because you're ready. I've been ready for a long time, and it hasn't happened.

Maybe it never will.

That thought leaves me cold and I push it forcefully away, drying my hands with more vigor than necessary on a nearby dish cloth. I grin at Jack and Pete, offer to open a bottle of the red to let it breathe before dinner.

Pete comes over while Beck and Jack consult over the timing of the meal. "Hey man," he says, giving me a warm hug. "Thanks for coming. I really want you to meet Ivy."

"She new to town?" I ask.

"Been here about a year, I think. She and her boyfriend moved from England."

"British?"

"Sort of. I think Ivy grew up between New York and London and the boyfriend's dad is British, but his mom is American. I think they both have dual citizenship."

"Interesting."

"She's intimidating. But I want her for the board. She's

a sculptor, and she's really good, and she has experience working with other nonprofits. Plus, she has some kind of family money."

"Sounds like the perfect fit." Rosedale is full of artists, but not necessarily ones with spare cash to throw support at the Art Center. A board position there usually entails donating something significant to the organization. Pete fits the bill. He started volunteering there, then became a drawing teacher, but when Super Rupert, the middle grade illustrated novel series that Jack writes and Pete illustrates, went big time with a popular TV show based on it, and Pete's original art also started selling, he suddenly had the means to support the Art Center rather than the other way around.

"Yeah. I've approached her about it obliquely, but she didn't exactly jump at the idea. I thought if we hung out and included her and her boyfriend—he's an artist, too—in a social way, it might make her more open to the idea."

"Makes sense. Only been here a year—maybe they haven't made friends yet."

"Toby, that's her boyfriend, has been to some events at the Art Center, but they do kind of keep to themselves."

"Well, allow me to draw them out," I say, glad to have a task to distract me from my personal woes.

Pete looks relieved. "Thanks. You're better at that kind of thing than me."

I pat his arm reassuringly. "Never fear. Between Beck and me, we can make friends with an angry dog."

"She's not angry, just beautiful and classy and intimidating. She kind of gives off Zoe Saldaña vibes."

I smile at my friend's expression, which has gone back to pinched with nerves. "Pete, she's just a person."

The doorbell chimes, echoing throughout the kitchen. The voices around me fall silent and we all look around as if waiting for someone to do something.

"I'll open the door," Jack announces. He wipes his hands on his jeans and straightens the cuffs of the hunter green cashmere sweater I gave him for Christmas. The boy needs help dressing.

"I'll put on some music," Beck says, taking out his phone.

"I'll get another beer," Van says, heading for the fridge.

"I'll open the wine," I say, grabbing the opener.

"And I'll—" Pete stops, looks lost.

I laugh. "Lighten up. It's a dinner party, not a sales pitch."

"Right, right." He smiles at me. "You're the best, Kingston."

"I know." I whip the cork out of the bottle with a satisfying pop as Jack returns to the kitchen with guests in tow.

My gaze lands on the woman, who must be Ivy Miller. She's probably early thirties, tall, almost as tall as my five-eleven, though a glance at her feet readjusts my estimate since she's wearing suede boots with heels. Pete didn't exaggerate—she's beautiful, with regal posture, creamy brown skin, straight nose, full lips. Her close-clipped dark hair exposes the lines of her swan's neck and her loose brown knit sweater shows off a well-defined collarbone. She could be a model. Designer jeans that hug her slim hips and chunky jewelry at her wrists and ears complete the look of relaxed elegance. I approve of her style—bohemian but in a polished way.

Jack's making introductions, which I mostly tune out while I evaluate Ivy's companion. Her boyfriend, who Pete referred to as Toby, stands a foot behind her, still halfway in the hallway. I have to step forward to get a good look. When I see his face, I find myself glancing away immediately, as if averting my eyes from the sun or a celebrity who happens to be eating a table away. Ivy is beautiful, but this man is *stunning*.

His complexion is light, not merely fair, but tinted with a kind of glowing light from within, as if he'd been painted in those egg white temperas favored by Raphael that make the subject look smooth and alive. But he's not a painting, he's a man, flesh and blood, his full mouth and his light eyes rivaling for my attention. They should be blue, to go with the buttery blond of his lightly curled hair, but they're actually amber, like a cat's eyes. It's hard to say how old he is, but I'd guess at least thirty. His nose is perfectly proportional to the rest of him, uncaringly generous.

I blink and force myself to look away from his face to inspect the rest of him. He's dressed casually, but not in the carelessly monied way that Ivy is. He's wearing a plain white button-down that looks like he got it off the rack at an off-brand department store. He's unbuttoned one button more than the weather calls for, added a shabby tweed sport coat on top, khaki slacks and brown loafers with... my stomach curdles at the sight: white athletic socks.

So the guy dresses worse than Jack. With a face like

his, he could probably wear a wetsuit to Le Bernardin and not be turned away.

"...and this is our friend Kingston James," Pete says. I edge closer so I can offer a hand to Ivy first. I do my signature move—gently turning her hand over and bowing over it instead of a straight handshake. "Charmed, Miss Miller," I say.

She laughs lightly, "Pleased to meet you, Mr. James." Her accent is faint, but there.

Toby puts his hand out for a shake, and I hesitate only a second before grasping it and pumping firmly. We make eye contact as he says, "I'm Toby Wheaton. How do you do?"

"Fine," I say, my gaze sliding away, all of my usual clever rejoinders eluding my tongue as I register the warmth of his dry, strong hand. "I do fine."

In my peripheral vision, I can see his smile. The crease of his cheeks makes the rosé in my stomach feel like a gin fizz.

"That's... fine," he says brightly, dropping my hand. Jack and Pete go about getting the newcomers drinks and I stand there, feeling like I've fallen down an elevator shaft.

Of course, the man I'd have this kind of reaction to—instant, electric, and undeniable—would already be taken.

THREE

BY THE TIME we all take our drinks and file into the seldom-used dining room, I've mostly recovered my equilibrium. Toby Wheaton may have struck my heart with an unexpected arrow of intrigue, but he's just a man. A man with a girlfriend. And I promised Pete that I'd charm Ivy into board duty, or at least try.

But somehow I end up seated next to him, with Van on my left, and Ivy across the table in front of Van, with Pete on the end between them. Beck's in front of me, and Jack's across from Toby. Beck immediately serves the risotto and baked fish he pulled crispy hot out of the oven, while Jack passes a basket with crusty sourdough he picked up from Stacy Robinson, a local baker. A delicate baby greens salad completes the meal.

"This is lovely," Toby says. He's got an accent, too, familiar to me from my trips to the London Book Fair over the years. "Who made all of these wonderful things?"

"I made everything but the bread," Beck says proudly.

"That's Stacy's. She has a booth at the farmer's market if you want to check it out."

"I want to make a toast," Pete says, the nerves he showed earlier seemingly gone. "To spring, which after a long winter has finally come to Rosedale. And to new friends," he says, tipping his glass first to Ivy, then Toby.

"Hear, hear," I add, as we clink glasses around the table. I tap mine against Toby's last, and our eyes meet again. Again, I have the urge to look away immediately. But why? I'm no retiring wallflower. Still, there's something about him that makes me feel too conspicuous to be my usual flamboyant self.

I'm so unsettled, I've apparently lost my appetite, too. I pick at my meal and try to follow the threads of conversation.

"I heard you're working on a new commission," Jack says, and at first, I think he's talking to me, but his eyes are on Toby.

"Finishing one up, actually," Toby answers. "Ivy had to pry me out of my studio today. I haven't been anywhere in a week."

"I'd apologize, except I know how important it is to get out of the creativity cave once in a while," Jack says. "Can you tell us about the painting?"

"It's of the Greystone Inn. They commissioned it for their hundred-year anniversary. I think they want to hang it in the lobby." He doesn't sound as if he's bragging, more like he's surprised at the prominent placement of his work.

"You accept commissions?" I ask. I wonder what his painting style is like.

"I do," he confirms, a little shyly. "If it's a good fit. But I actually like painting for hire. Things like the Greystone Inn are a nice palate cleanser from my usual stuff, and they keep me in oils and brushes."

"What's your usual stuff?" I don't know all that much about art, but I like to support local artists the way I like to support anything local. I have several pieces I bought on whims to decorate my apartment and my cottage, but I haven't collected with intent.

"I do oils," he says. "I cut my teeth on landscapes, but I love doing architectural painting. It's always a fun challenge to see if I can capture the spirit of a place and make it recognizable to those who know it best." He bites his pink bottom lip. "It's not that interesting to hear about, I'm afraid."

"To the contrary. I'm a words person, not a visual arts person," I say, forgetting to be tongue-tied by his beauty as I respond, "and I think it would be incredible to be able to capture something real in a painting."

"You're a writer?" Toby says, leaning back in his chair. His shirt tightens across his chest, and I can see the outline of his nipples through the thin fabric.

I swallow against a dry tongue. "Hardly. I leave the writing to the professionals." I point at Jack, who smiles. "No, my job is to badger the publishers to pay my writers what they deserve, then badger the writers to turn in their work. Come to think of it, I do a lot of badgering."

"And you're the best badgerer there is," Jack says. He looks at Toby. "Pete and I would be renting a third-floor walk-up in the city if not for Kingston here."

Toby looks around the nicely appointed room in their

lovely Cape-style house and raises his eyebrows at me. "You must be a very good badgerer, indeed."

"Now what you need is a badgerer of your own," Jack says. "Have you talked to Pete about meeting with his art agent?"

Toby shakes his head briskly. "No, I wouldn't want to bother him about that."

"Dude, he wouldn't mind at all making an introduction," Jack says decisively. "And Fernanda is really terrific. A killer, but terrific."

"Fernanda Ruiz? She's Pete's art agent?" Toby says, as if the name means something to him.

I've met the woman once or twice at events, and she is formidable. You have to have a thick skin and sharp instincts to make it in the art world, from what I understand—it may be even worse than publishing.

"You know her?" Jack asks.

"Of her. She's kind of a legend. And I'm not ready—"

"I've seen your stuff," Jack interrupts. "It's astonishing."

Jack's vehemence surprises me. He's gotten more interested in art, I noticed, since his and Pete's honeymoon in which they hit up every museum in western Europe and a fair number in eastern Europe as well. I know Pete's always going to be his favorite artist, but Toby must have some talent for Jack to be in his corner.

"Thanks," Toby says quietly. He looks at his plate. "Ivy and I came here to work, and we've been working. I've never been so productive, in fact. But I didn't expect to get my bluff called this soon."

"What do you mean?" I ask.

"Every art school kid has ambitions for gallery shows and big-name buyers, fame and fortune. It's what we're supposed to want. I'm at the stage where I either have to shit or get off the pot, to borrow a phrase, and I thought it would be easier to... well, shit."

Hearing the crass expression come from his handsome face and in his London accent makes me laugh. "You are something, Toby," I say. "But I know a bit about artists with unrealized ambitions. You don't want to have any regrets."

Our gazes lock again, and this time I don't look away.

"I try not to," he murmurs, and I can't stop my gaze from dropping to his mouth for a split second before returning to his amber eyes.

"It's a personal policy of mine as well," I say, forcing myself to act the part of... myself. Myself when I'm not mesmerized by a British painter with a face I know is going to appear in my dreams tonight. "No regrets."

"To no regrets," Jack says, lifting his glass in a second toast for our end of the table.

"No regrets," Toby repeats, clinking our glasses together again.

I drain my wine in a long gulp. It's easy enough to say and quite another thing to actually do.

AFTER DINNER, we move back to the kitchen, where Beck slices a raspberry tart. We switch to herbal tea and the mood shifts as Pete brings Ivy to sit on the blue leather barstool next to me. He gives me a significant look and pointedly wanders away.

"I'm sorry we haven't gotten a chance to chat more," she says. "Pete says your people are Jamaican?"

"Grandparents on both sides," I confirm. "I give you one guess as to where they hailed from."

She smiles. "My mother's family is from Boscobel. Dad was a Londoner. I grew up between Queens and the West End. Like Toby. We're hybrids."

"London's one of my favorite cities," I say. "I'd love to spend more time there."

"It's incredible, but overwhelming sometimes," she says.

"Sounds familiar," I say lightly. "I'm in Manhattan most of the week and here on the weekends."

"I wondered why we hadn't run into each other before now. I would have remembered meeting you," she says. "But then, Toby and I have been hunkered down all winter working."

"Pete says you're a sculptor."

She nods. "I do bronze casting, mostly. Small pieces. It's a hobby, really. Not like Toby. He's been making a living at it for a while—a modest living, but still. Sky's the limit for that one, if he could get out of his own way."

"I'd like to see your stuff," I say, not taking her obvious cue to move off the topic of her work.

"You're sweet. Everyone here is sweet," she says, looking around at the rest of the men in the room. "And handsome, and clearly besotted with their partners." She sighs, and I wonder if I detect a bit of wistfulness in it. She glances across the kitchen to where Toby's smiling at something Van's telling him—the tines of his dessert fork pressed against his bottom lip as he listens.

"How long have you been together?" I ask, wincing internally the second the question comes out of my mouth. Why should I care?

"Forever," she says, a lopsided grin on her mouth as she returns her attention to me. "Since art school," she adds, getting more specific. "So... about a decade? Yeah, I'll be thirty-two—yikes—this year, so ten years. I did undergrad in the States, then got into the RCA."

"RCA?"

"Royal College of Art," she explains. "We met the first day, but it took ages of me dropping hints before he finally asked me out. After that... it was easy." She looks at Toby again, with a strange expression on her face. "Anyway," she turns back to me, her voice brisk, "Toby's dad is an artist, too—Nathan Wheaton." She says the name like it's supposed to mean something to me. "Toby almost didn't go to the RCA because he thought they only let him in because of his dad, but he's actually got that one-in-a-million spark. Anyone who sees his work can tell right away. He's the only one who doesn't seem to believe it."

I'm intensely curious to see if I can see this spark in Toby's work. My reaction to the man would seem to indicate his art would hit me the same way. I shiver and focus on his girlfriend. "Why Rosedale, after London? Or were you just looking for its opposite?"

"Probably for similar reasons why you split your time between here and Manhattan. Cities are exciting, but exhausting. We wanted a break from city life, but I thought Toby should stay near an art hub, too. Not that I can get him to meet with anybody about representing him.

But I know Pete has connections, so when he invited us tonight, I made Toby come, too."

"You know Pete wants you for the Art Center board, right?"

"Yes. I'm thinking about it." She turns her chunky amethyst bracelet around her delicate wrist. She clearly has independent means if she can wear gems like that and do sculpture as a hobby. "Pete seems like a good person."

"I don't know anyone better," I say gravely.

"I should probably do it," she says. "Though I abhor volunteering."

"There are perks," I say. "You get to attend all the board meetings and fundraisers and judge the summer student art show." Ivy's not stupid; she knows what she'd be getting herself into.

"Goody," she says flatly, then narrows her eyes at me. "How did you end up in Rosedale?"

"A happy accident. Took a drive, passed through town, and fell in love at first sight."

She holds my gaze steadily. "You fall in love at first sight often?"

It takes effort not to look away. Not to look at Toby. At her boyfriend. "Once in a while," I say mildly. "Rosedale turned out to be the happiest of accidents. It used to be my escape from the city, still is, but after Pete and Jack moved here, it became a real community. And if you let them bring you into it, you won't regret it."

She hums noncommittally. "You should come by our place tomorrow. I'll show you my bronzes and you can see Toby's work, too, if he'll let us into the studio. Bring Pete."

I can see the angles she's working. She'll entertain the

board position if Pete considers using his connections for Toby. I play the buffer and everyone ends up happy. My skin itches at the idea of spending more time with this beautiful pair of artists, but I can't refuse—I'd be a terrible friend to Pete if I did. And maybe with exposure, my oddly intense reaction to Toby Wheaton will fade away.

"I'd be delighted."

FOUR

IT'S COOLER SATURDAY, and I keep the top up on my convertible. I pick up Pete from his place, then find Ivy and Toby's house with help from my map app. They're on the Art Center side of town, on a dead-end, tree-lined street called Ashby Lane. I keep a pretty close eye on Rosedale real estate as a hobby and don't remember this house going on the market, so I assume it's a rental.

It's just after noon when we pull into their short drive-way. I park behind a modern silver hybrid and a boxy station wagon that's mostly white and at least thirty years old. It's not difficult to identify the efficient, stylish car as Ivy's while assigning ownership of the rusty wagon to her other half.

I adjust the paisley scarf I added to my outfit at the last minute. This morning I struggled over what to wear and ended up in a less fancy version of what I had on last night: faun colored pants, white shirt, velvet jacket. Pete's wearing jeans and a sweater, matching Ivy's casual duds when she answers our knock.

"Come on in," she says, leaving the door open for us to follow her into the spare, minimalist entryway of the medium-sized post-war colonial. She offers us coffee or tea, but I opt for water. I had my fill of coffee this morning while lounging in my armchair, reading for pleasure and trying to ignore the fact that I was going to see Toby again.

It doesn't matter that he makes my stomach ache and my breathing shallow and that I did, indeed, see his face even after I closed my eyes last night. He's Ivy's, he's been Ivy's for years. I'll simply ignore my inconvenient feelings and make friends with the most attractive man I've ever met.

"Toby's in his studio," she says, after we sip our drinks and make small talk. "Do you want to see mine first?"

"Yes," Pete says enthusiastically, and I know he's not simply trying to flatter her. "Please."

Ivy takes us to what must have been intended as a guest bedroom but now contains three worktables and no bed. One table holds a block of clay and sharp-looking tools in neat round buckets. The second seems to be where her work-in-progress is, a horse, by the looks of it, taking shape out of rust-colored clay. The third has finished pieces, not clay at all, but dark metal, polished to a shine. I see a bird taking flight, and another horse, galloping with its mane flowing as if cutting through an invisible wind. There's a tarantula, too, mid-climb over a rock. Very weird and interesting.

"I've always wondered how it works—you sculpt in clay first, and then what?" Pete asks.

"Yes, I make a mold of the clay piece in silicone. That's how you can make multiple castings of the same piece.

Then I cut the mold away from the clay, which gets repurposed for another piece. The next step is to melt the bronze down and pour it into the mold. After it cools, I remove the mold and bronze remains. There's more technicality to it, but that's the gist. I can't pour the bronze here because it's too much of a fire hazard, but the Art Center has a facility, so I don't have to go far. It's another reason I chose Rosedale."

Pete inspects the clay horse-in-progress. "You like to sculpt animals?"

"Mainly," Ivy says.

"I'm digging the tarantula," I say. "It's so unexpected."

She grins. "That's a personal favorite of mine as well. My nephew gave me the idea—I gave him one for his tenth birthday and I have officially become the coolest auntie."

We talk about her process for a while, but I'm wondering why she's not putting her stuff out in the world. "You know there's probably a market for these," I say.

"Definitely," Pete adds. "These birds are incredible. Are they hummingbirds?" On a pedestal in a sunny corner there's a collection of tiny, delicate birds with long tail feathers and curved beaks, all in various stages of flight.

"Those are doctor birds—native to Jamaica. Streamertails is another name for them."

"Gorgeous," Pete murmurs. "Would you part with one? My sister is obsessed with hummingbirds."

Ivy looks somewhat surprised, but then she nods decisively. "Sure." She turns to me. "Kingston, would you go get Toby for lunch? He's in his studio in the back. Pete and I can talk terms."

She gives me a small smile and I know she wants to get

Pete alone to talk business. Still, I hesitate. "He won't mind my just showing up?"

"Oh, he might be a bit stroppy, but it'll pass. Go out the kitchen door and you'll see it."

Part of me wants to turn down the assignment, but an encouraging gesture from Pete prompts me to agree. "All right."

I leave them to it, retrace our steps to the kitchen, and go out the back door. The day is still chilly, but sunny. Short buttery daffodils bloom on the edge of a walkway that leads to a detached garage with sliding barn doors. The main entrance is shut, but a second door on the side is cracked open. I gather my courage, which falters when I remember I'm going to see Toby again.

I shake myself severely, smooth the front of my shirt, and defiantly stick my hands in my jacket pockets, summoning my usual air of competence. I'm Kingston James. I don't get nervous around *boys*.

Of course, I have to take one hand out of my pocket almost immediately so I can rap on the open door.

"Hello?" I call inside.

Grumbling can be heard before the door wrenches all the way open.

"What?" Toby barks. He's wearing a black moth-eaten sweater made of more holes than fabric, a white T-shirt that shows through the Swiss cheese pattern, and loose jeans with smears of white paint all along the front. The shabby clothes reinforce my theory from last night that the clothes, in this case, don't make the man. Despite the attire, he's even more handsome today, his hair an uncombed mop, irregular blond stubble on his chin and cheeks. The man won the genetic jackpot and my response to him is no less strong, more's the pity.

"Oh, it's you," he says, his defensively raised shoulders relaxing. "Sorry. I was wrestling with some truculent tubes of paint."

"I don't mean to bother you. Ivy wants us to come in for lunch in a minute," I say, delivering my message while peering curiously around the inside of the garage—studio, Ivy had called it, and the name fits. No cars could fit here, not with the drafting table covered in paints and brushes and glossy 4x6 photos, and several large easels, one empty, two holding canvases.

But those aren't the only canvases I see. No, there are easily a hundred or more propped up against the walls and a chest of drawers, with smaller ones stacked on a built-in countertop. They all seem to be finished, though the way they're arranged makes it impossible to see the subjects of more than a few.

But the ones I can see take my breath away. Saturated colors, impressive technique. I don't have to have an art degree to know that Toby's got complete command of his brush. So to speak.

"Do you mind?" I step fully into the space and put my hand back in my pocket lest I reach out and touch something I'm not supposed to.

"Um, yeah, sure. It's fine," Toby says. He's not reluctant, exactly, but he doesn't sound all that certain about letting me in. "Ivy mentioned you and Pete were coming over. I lost track of time. I tend to do that when I'm working."

"Not a problem," I say, wondering where to start.

"That's the Greystone." I point at one of the works on the easels.

"Yes, finishing it up in the next couple of days hopefully," he says. His chuckle sounds forced. "Guess it's good that you can tell what it's supposed to be."

How could I not recognize the iconic Rosedale building, especially the way Toby's painted it? It's not quite photo-realistic, but there's something more real than real about it. It's as if he's breathed actual life into the static picture via paint texture and brushstrokes. It's an accurate representation of the building, down to its wide gray stone front steps, and it feels like you could almost step right into the painting and onto those steps, to live in the gorgeous world he created out of pigment.

"Toby." His name comes to my lips before I can stop it. It feels oddly good to form the word, so I say it again, "Toby. This is staggeringly good."

"Oh." He rubs his hand on the back of his neck and shrugs. "Thanks." On someone else, the modesty would be an affectation, but on him, it's genuine, making him even more sweetly adorable. God, I am in so much trouble here. But again, my mouth opens and words pour out before I can stop myself.

"You have to come paint my cottage," I say quickly. "I'll pay twice your normal fee. I must have a Toby Wheaton on my walls."

He blinks at me. "Just like that? You don't even know what I charge."

"Whatever it is, it's not enough. Say you'll do it." I know how to get what I want. Most of the time. I can't have him—I know I can't. He's Ivy's.

But I could have a piece of him.

Suddenly, he grins, and it changes his entire demeanor from insecure artist to playful pretty boy. "Is this you badgering me, Kingston?"

The sound of him saying my name brings instant goosebumps to my arms. Or maybe my jacket just isn't warm enough for the day. The studio is cold, too. I see a space heater in a corner, but it's not on. I can't help the shudder that undulates down my spine.

"It's chilly out here," he says, perhaps noting my shiver. "We can go in."

"Wait—show me more?" I ask quickly.

Instantly, he retreats back to insecure artist. "Oh, this place is such a mess and I—"

"This one." I point to the canvas nearest me, a landscape of an icy blue beach, crashing waves, and dramatic cliffs. "Tell me about this one."

"That's the Isle of Wight. Ivy and I went there a couple of years ago. Quite near the town of Kingston, actually." He smiles at me full-on, and I swear I feel a little dizzy.

I clear my throat. "Do you always paint from life?"

"Generally, yes. I take photos and use them for reference." He files through a nearby stack of six or so canvases, pulls out a large square one. "Here's something that came out of my head, though."

It's another landscape, but of no place I've ever seen, a winding stream and a tiny fairy cottage hidden away in a jungle of flowers. "Beautiful," I murmur, the word so far from adequate I'm almost embarrassed to use it. "You could illustrate fantasy in a heartbeat."

He cocks his head, sets the painting down. "Jack said the same thing the other day."

"If you wanted to get into it, I could give you some names."

His forehead creases. "You just met me and you want me to do a painting for you and introduce me to your contacts?"

"Decisive is one of my better qualities."

His warm laugh makes me forget the chill of the room. "I'll think about it."

"No pressure. Except about the painting of my house. That I definitely want. What do you do first? Take pictures?"

He laughs again, louder. It echoes off the hard walls. "Let's go have lunch and we'll talk."

I let him off the hook, for now, and he shuts the door to the studio firmly behind us. On the way back to the house, he asks where I live.

"Bramble Street. About half a mile past Pete's house."

"And you split your time in the city?"

"Have to go back Monday," I say, realizing the weekend is slipping by quickly and I haven't yet had a chance to talk to Jack about my business plans.

"You don't work from home?" he asks as he opens the kitchen door for me to walk through first. A gentleman through and through.

"Sometimes. But I find I get better results when I'm available for in-person meetings and lunches. People have a hard time saying no to me when we're face-to-face. I use it to my advantage."

He passes close to me on his way to the sink, glancing at me briefly. "I can imagine."

If we weren't standing in the house he shares with his beautiful girlfriend, I could almost pretend he's flirting with me.

He washes his hands and Pete and Ivy join us from her workroom. They seem to have come to some kind of arrangement, because Pete seems more relaxed. Ivy moves to stand next to Toby with the easy familiarity of long-term lovers. The stab of jealousy and longing that hits my gut makes me turn away. It shouldn't hurt to see them together, but it does. What is my problem? I literally only met the man last night. What does my heart think it's doing by falling for a guy it can't have? *Bad heart. No romance for you.*

"So, lunch?" Ivy asks.

"Great," Pete says enthusiastically. "Can we help?"

Ivy graciously lets Pete put napkins and silverware on the charmingly distressed round wooden kitchen table while she arranges sandwiches on plates. Toby fills the kettle with water and offers me a selection of tea bags. I pick something herbal. I don't need to be even more on edge around him.

I try to relax as we take seats around the table. Luckily, Ivy and Toby don't seem to be one of those touchy-feely couples who are all over each other (cough, Jack and Pete, cough) but they have a shared ease that's enviable. Ivy said they'd been together for what—a decade? That puts any relationship I've ever been in to shame. Even Jack and Pete have only been together for about four years. Not that it's a competition.

The sandwiches are tasty and we chat about the weather, each of us ready for the change of season. Pete tells us about the tulips he bought from the flower shop in town last fall that are starting to come up in his and Jack's backyard. As we're finishing up, a short-haired cat, entirely black except for a smudge of white on its chest, with round green eyes, trots into the room. It ignores the four humans at the table in its quest for a place to curl up, which it finds on a rag rug that's the landing spot for a beam of sunlight streaming through the kitchen window.

"Who's that?" I ask, nodding at the beast. I've always considered myself a dog person, but this cat is undeniably a character.

"That's Luna," Toby answers. "She adopted us when we moved here."

Ivy rolls her eyes. "You mean she conned you into adopting her."

"She was the last one left," Toby says defensively, as if he's had to make this argument a number of times before. "I couldn't let them take her to the shelter." He looks beseechingly at Pete, then me. "She was the last of a litter that a family was giving away outside the supermarket one day. I honestly couldn't say no."

"She looked at you with her big eyes and you melted," Ivy grumbles, but she doesn't sound truly upset.

Toby grins at his girlfriend. "What can I say? I'm a soft touch for big, beautiful eyes."

It's honestly adorable, except that instead of responding to the compliment, Ivy pushes back from the table hurriedly. "I have some biscuits if anyone wants something sweet."

"If by biscuits you mean cookies, I'm interested," Pete says.

Toby says nothing, and I wonder if I'm imagining the tension between them. Perhaps it's not all paradise for him and Ivy. Not that it matters. He's given no indication of being anything besides straight.

Maybe it's time to leave. I decline the cookies—store-bought, not Beck's, and therefore not worth eating—but Pete munches on two, bottomless pit that he is, all six-foot-whatever with a metabolism to match.

"Thank you for showing us your work," I say. "Toby, take my number and we can set up a time for you to come take pictures."

"Take pictures?" Ivy asks.

"Toby's going to do a painting for me. Of my cottage," I say breezily.

"He is?" She sounds skeptical.

"Apparently." Toby's tone is dry, but he sends me a small smile. "You better take my number instead and text me yours. I couldn't find my phone this morning, but I'm sure it'll turn up."

I whip out my phone from my trouser pocket and carefully type in the numbers he gives me, then text him immediately.

This is Kingston James.

A stack of magazines on the kitchen counter rings shrilly in response.

"Ah, there it is," Toby says, fishing a black cell phone

from out between creased copies of *Architectural Digest* and the *New Yorker*. "Thanks, Kingston."

"Happy to be of service," I reply.

He fiddles with the phone for a moment and then my phone, still in my hand, buzzes.

I look down to see the answering text.

This is Tobias Eric Wheaton.

I have no idea why he gave me his full name, but I carefully copy and paste it into my contacts before we say goodbye. Pete's full of excitement over Ivy's sculptures. "She's being modest—she's talked to some dealers in London, but nothing ever worked out. I'm calling Fernanda when I get home. She'll know what to do."

AFTER DROPPING PETE OFF, I go home and putter around and try not to think about how my exposure therapy to Toby today backfired. Now that I've seen his work, I only find him more attractive, not less.

Part of me wonders if I've just been so lonely lately that I latched onto the first guy to turn my head in a while. If so, having him over won't be a big deal, because these feelings aren't real. And when I get back to the city, I could try hooking up. Or not. I don't have to have sex with someone to prove I'm not into Tobias Eric Wheaton.

FIVE

THE NEXT AFTERNOON Jack and I agree to meet up at Hot Brew, the coffee shop that anchors the middle of Main Street. I get there first and order a chai from Ruth. Someone's sitting at Jack's favorite table by the window, so I stand near the counter while I wait. Jack appears a moment later, dressed in sneakers and joggers. He nods at me in acknowledgment, orders, then looks at the occupied table and raises his eyebrows as if to ask me, "What the hell?"

I shrug. He doesn't actually own the place. I point to an empty table in the corner, and he slowly walks there.

"The nerve of some people," I say mildly.

"Tell me about it," he says, without heat. "So, what's up?"

"You're all business today."

"I'm a little tired. Pete couldn't stop talking about Ivy and Toby last night. He's all fired up about getting them in touch with Fernanda—both of them."

"Good." They both have talent, smarts, and a ready-to-go body of work. Any agent would be lucky to take them on.

"What did you think of them?" he asks.

I have to consider how to respond. "Ivy is formidable, and her work really was surprising and accessible. Not that I'm an expert."

"Well, you know quality," he says.

"True. I do have unimpeachable taste."

He doesn't respond to that. "And Toby's stuff? What did you think?"

Jack frowns at me when I don't respond right away, not knowing how to put it into words.

"You don't like his work?" he asks, sounding confused.

"No—it's sensational. He has, as Ivy describes it, a spark."

"But?"

"No buts. He should be selling out shows within a year, especially with someone like Fernanda guiding him. But before he blows up, I've asked him to do my cottage."

"Oh." Jack sits back in his chair, his face lighting up. "That's an amazing idea. Why didn't I think of that? Do you think he'd do our place? How much does he charge? Never mind, it doesn't matter. How long does it take? Probably too soon to get it done for Pete's birthday, right? That's not until July. Maybe if I paid extra?"

"Hold up," I say stoutly. "And get in line. He likes you and Pete, so he'll probably do it. But mine first."

Jack waves away my protest. "Fine. But that's not what you wanted to talk about, is it?"

I've known Pete longer than Jack, but Jack's more tuned into the publishing world. I'd also trust him with my life, so I know if I run some semi-confidential things by him, he won't breathe a word. The publishing industry can be a gossipy place.

"It's not." Before I tell him what's on my mind, I see that Teddy, the barista working today, has set our drinks on the counter, so I get up to collect them. I place Jack's in front of him, then carefully smell my chai, the spices warming me.

"What do you think about me leaving Fenster and putting up my own shingle? Would you like to be a client of the Kingston James Literary Agency? It has a nice ring, doesn't it?"

The swiftness with which the grin breaks out on Jack's face quells my tendril of doubt that he wouldn't like the idea.

"It's about damn time," he says. "I know you've done well there, but you are so ready to go out on your own."

"I think so," I say, questions over the feasibility of the endeavor returning. "I know I'm ready for a challenge."

"You're bored."

I hadn't quite considered it like that. "You think?"

"I know you. You've been on autopilot for a while. This will be good for you." Jack sips his Americano, perfectly relaxed in the aftermath of what I thought might be more of a bombshell.

His matter-of-fact assessment, putting into so few words what I've been struggling with internally, makes me feel both seen by him and annoyed that it seems so easy for him to articulate my recent mood. But in the end, he wants what's best for me, and his support is reassuring.

"I'm glad you think so."

"So what's next? Leasing some big fancy office in Midtown Manhattan?"

"I was thinking first I should put together a slate of agents," I say. "Do you know anything about Stephanie Collier?"

"Yeah, she's Sylvie Simon's agent. She loves her. Want me to talk to Sylvie and feel her out?" Sylvie Simon is a bestselling young adult author, and exactly the kind of name that would make this move splashy, which is usually how I like it.

"How do you know Sylvie?"

"We were both on a panel at the New York Festival of Books a couple of years ago," Jack says. "She's wonderful."

"Don't talk to her yet. But I'll let you know."

"This is so exciting, Kingston," Jack says. "Though it kind of throws a wrench in you spending more time in Rosedale."

"Why?"

"Well, unless you're going to move to a fully remote operation, won't this mean you'll have to be in the city even more?"

"I guess so."

"Why don't you work from Rosedale more?" he asks. "I mean, you're usually here for a good chunk of the summer, when things slow down. But we'd love to see more of you. Unless you're having too much fun in the city without us. Seeing anyone lately?"

"Van asked me the same question the other night. Why is everyone so concerned with my dating status?" If I sound defensive, it's because I totally am.

"Hey, not trying to offend. It's been a while since

Sergio moved and I haven't noticed you with anyone since then."

"I—" I'm not sure what to say. Again, I know he only wants the best for me, but I'm chagrined to realize that while I'm perfectly fine sticking my nose into my friends' love lives when called for, them trying to do the same makes me prickly as a hedgehog. "Don't worry about me," I finally say. "I'm doing okay."

"All right," Jack says neutrally. "You know I'm always here to talk, though, right?"

"Of course."

"You don't always have to be the calm, collected one, you know. You're allowed to have problems, too."

Now I am getting uncomfortable. I'm not used to Jack calling me out or pressing this hard. Usually, he lets me get away with my jaunty know-it-all vibe.

I swallow down a sharp lump that's unexpectedly appeared in my throat. I can't think of how to express what Jack's friendship means to me. For someone who consumes as many words as I do, I'm having a hard time putting them in order. Finally, I settle on, "Thanks, Jack," my voice embarrassingly husky.

But he doesn't make fun of me for my weak-sauce reply. He smiles and pats my arm and we go on to talk about frivolous topics like the new vegetarian restaurant opening in Millville and the state of world affairs.

I get a text as we're saying our goodbyes, and my pulse immediately kicks up when I see who it's from.

If you still want me to come take photographs, I could do it this coming Saturday.

I don't hesitate and rip off an instant reply.

Anytime. Looking forward to it.

Damn. Was that too enthusiastic? I frown down at the phone.

Jack looks at me, a concerned expression on his face. "What's up? Everything good with your mom?"

"She's doing fine, thanks. It's something else."

"Remember, you can talk to me," Jack says, putting an arm on my shoulder.

I appreciate the sentiment, but I can't tell him that I have a crush on a probably straight guy in a serious relationship. "Thanks, Jack. Everything's completely chill."

He gives me a doubtful look, but lets it slide. Now I just have to make it to Saturday without blowing Toby's visit all out of proportion.

SIX

AS SOON AS I get back to the city on Monday, work explodes—two contract negotiations encounter major snags, then I have to work out reparations from a publisher over a printing error. All in all, I'm too busy to spiral about Toby, which is probably for the best. By Friday, it's also clear I'll be too swamped catching up on work this weekend to make it to Rosedale. I text Toby.

> Not going to be in Rosedale tomorrow, after all. Can we push our appointment by a week?

He writes back hours later as I'm about to drop dead asleep, but when I see the name on my notifications, I'm suddenly wide awake.

> Not a problem. Sorry for the belated reply. Lost my phone (again).

I grin, imagining his melodious voice saying the words and type back.

> Did you find it in a stack of newspapers?
> Or the cat food bin, perhaps?

There's a slight delay before his response, enough time for me to wonder if we're not good enough acquaintances for me to joke with him over text. But then—

> In the fruit bowl. Not sure how it got
> there, tbh.

I laugh, the sound echoing in my sparsely decorated bedroom. My New York apartment is much more minimalist than my place in Rosedale, where I've given up on any sort of order and have instead embraced a sort of bohemian baroqueness.

I'm debating continuing the conversation when he writes again.

> I turned in the painting to the Greystone
> today, so that's good timing to begin
> working on yours.

We haven't talked specific monetary terms yet, and my agent brain wants to get it all settled, but ten PM on a Friday night is not that time for that. Instead, I write—

> I'm sure they were blown away by it.
> Congratulations.

He writes back quickly.

> They did seem to like it, actually. Thanks.

I bite my lip as I read the response. I could leave it

there, get some much-needed sleep. I have to go into the office tomorrow morning, unusual for a Saturday, but necessary to catch up on some contracts I'd neglected while dealing with other fires this week. But then he writes again.

> Spring is in full swing around here. Are you going to want the picture to reflect that?

I hadn't thought about it, but he's right. The trees around my house are budding, not the fully leafy lushness that they'll be in summer, nor the crispy red-yellow-orange of autumn. It would be interesting to have a series, the four seasons, but though I'm more than comfortable, I'm not made of money. I'll have to be okay with one. And besides, I love spring.

> I think so. Spring is my favorite season.

His reply comes right away.

> Mine too. Who can resist renewal and rebirth?

> And so many things to look forward to as it warms up.

> Like what?

> Linen suits. Driving my Beamer with the top down. Inviting myself over to Jack and Pete's swimming pool.

> Do you celebrate Easter?

> In a secular way, sure.

> Ivy and I are having some folks over for an Easter brunch next weekend. You should come.

> Photos on Saturday, brunch on Sunday? It's a plan.

> Great. See you then.

> See you then.

He doesn't write back after that, and I reluctantly put my phone away after rereading the conversation three times. I need to let go of this crush. If Toby and I could become friends, that should be enough.

I fall into a restless sleep, because deep down, I know it won't be.

SEVEN

TOBY'S punctual for our photo session, which surprises me given his absent-minded artist routine I've witnessed. We've exchanged a few texts since that first night, to settle on terms for the commission, then most recently yesterday evening when I told him I'd safely arrived in Rosedale. He promised to meet me at my house at eleven.

It's exactly eleven when the knock sounds on my door. I'm caught slightly unawares, barefoot, mid-coffee. I've had a jumpy feeling in my stomach since waking up, similar to the sensation of being about to take an important exam you haven't studied for.

What is the big deal—I should be able to deal with the man. He's an artist, not a chemistry test, I remind myself. I open the door, and all that positive self-talk flies out of my head. I could probably manage if he wasn't so damn perfect. He's not hot like a gym bunny or an oiled fifties pinup, but when he blinks those long-lashed amber eyes at me, I forget how to string two words together. And reticence has never been an issue for me.

"Kingston, hey," he says when I don't speak. His gaze slides down my body to my bare feet and back up to my face. "I was wondering if I'd ever see you in anything less formal than pleated trousers."

I'm wearing my lazy weekend clothes, loose gray sweats made from cotton softer than a dandelion seed, a white T-shirt (designer, of course), and a loose overshirt, unbuttoned, in a blocky black-and-white pattern. I haven't bothered pulling my hair back and my locs hang loose—the ends brushing my shoulders.

Toby's wearing the jeans I remember from my visit to his studio and another black sweater, but this one doesn't have any holes in it. Instead of loafers with white athletic socks, he's got on sneakers. With white athletic socks.

"Well, it's Saturday," I say, finding my voice and hoping it sounds normal.

"So it is. Lovely place you've got here."

I realize I haven't asked him in, just let him stand at my front door while taking inventory. *Get it together, James.*

"Thanks, come on in. I was just finishing my coffee. Would you like some?" The good host in me finally makes an appearance.

"No, thanks." He lifts a black camera bag. "Is it okay if I start taking pictures?"

"Of the inside?" I ask, passing him to lead the way into the living room.

"Of whatever," he says ambiguously, glancing around. "I tend to snap away obnoxiously, I'm afraid."

I wave my hand. "Then snap away."

He opens the bag and brings out a much smaller

camera than I expected. It's a black rectangle barely bigger than his palm.

"What kind of camera is that?"

"It's a Leica. German. It takes lovely pictures." He raises the camera and looks through the viewfinder at the bookshelf next to him, pushes a button at the top, and I hear a satisfying click. I only use the camera on my phone, and I have to fight the urge to take a picture of him taking pictures.

"It's not a film camera, right?"

"No, digital. I have a film one, an old-school Pentax. I thought when I first went to art school I'd study photography. It was hell to get them to change my focus once I realized it wasn't meant to be. But I still love taking pictures." He takes several more of different parts of the living room. I look around, trying to see what's so worth capturing on the camera's memory card. My faux-Tiffany reading lamp? The stack of unread bestsellers I'll never get around to?

"Why did you pick photography at first?"

"I was trying to differentiate myself from my father, I suppose. He was a painter, therefore I never would be," he says, sounding rueful. "Silly, but I was young, and I tended to make all my decisions in response to something I didn't want, when I should have been making them based on something I did want."

"Very wise."

"I am a decade older. I'd like to think I have some things figured out."

"Is your dad famous, then?" I remember Ivy mentioning him like he was a household name.

"In England, he's pretty well-known. Fairly successful.

But difficult." Toby's not looking at me, but at the watercolor of a lake I picked up at a Rosedale Art Center show a few years ago. "We're not—we don't get along well. What about you?"

There he goes, changing the subject off him again. "What about me?"

"What did you go to school for?"

"I was a business major, actually, with a minor in English."

"Then you always knew you wanted to be a book agent?"

"I knew I wanted to make money. And I liked books. When I analyzed the publishing industry, I decided it was the job best suited to me. It's a bonkers industry, really. I've made it work."

"So analytical, Kingston, you surprise me. I thought you were a creative at heart."

I laugh. "I have good instincts, strong opinions, and flawless taste. None of those I learned in school, but I knew I had to pair my strengths with practicality."

"You never wanted to write?" Toby asks, lifting the camera again to look out the front window toward his station wagon, rusty and bulky compared to the sleek green machine parked next to it. I arrived late enough last night that I didn't bother pulling the Beamer onto the slab.

"I write all the time," I say. "Part of the job. But no, I never wanted to be an author."

"You're so impressive," he murmurs, clicking away without looking my way. "You seem to know exactly what you want. And what you don't want. I envy that."

I let myself bask in the compliment, even if I don't quite understand it. "You consider yourself indecisive?"

He laughs, lowers the camera, and looks at me dead-on. "I'd like to think of myself as unwilling to cut off possibilities. But I don't know—lately it feels more like cowardice than keeping my options open."

"Sometimes keeping one's options open is code for being scared to make a decision," I say without judgement.

"Ivy accused me of that the other day. She wants me to be excited about setting up a meeting with Pete's agent, about finally making my debut. And I keep dragging my heels."

"Why?"

He shrugs one shoulder elegantly. "Fear of failure?"

"But you have to know how good your paintings are. You're not stupid."

He looks at me, surprised that I might make such a personal claim. Well, he is being stupid if he thinks his work is lacking.

"I know how good they are," he says slowly. He looks down at his camera, fiddles with some of the buttons. "Fear of success, then."

"I've heard of such a thing," I say, folding my arms over my chest and rocking back on my heels, "but I've never observed it in real life."

"Success turned my dad into an asshole. An entitled, womanizing, greedy asshole. I can't let that happen to me. I've spent my entire life trying not to be like him. Except, of course, when I wanted to be exactly like him."

The sadness in his voice hits me hard. I know something about wanting to be like someone and unlike them at the same time.

"My dad wasn't an asshole," I offer. "He wasn't a successful man, either. He died when I was ten because he wouldn't take an afternoon off his hourly wage job to see a doctor. A cold that turned into pneumonia killed him at fifty. I never wanted to be like him—living paycheck to paycheck, raising two kids on a shoestring." I sigh and let myself feel the pain of missing him for a moment. "But then again, I wanted to be exactly like him. Loved by his family, his community." I wonder how real to get, then remember his exhortation—no regrets. "My mom and sister live down in Georgia and I don't have a family of my own. I have a sweet car, though. An apartment in the city, this place." I pause. "I wonder sometimes if he'd be proud of me, or sad for me."

I worry in the silence after my little overshare that I've made Toby so uncomfortable that he'll leave, but he just lifts the camera to his eyes and takes a picture. Of me.

I shake my head. "Not me—the house. And the outside of it, at that."

He lowers the camera again, smiles. "I know. I just thought you should see how you looked right then. Your heart was on your face. Beautiful."

He presses some buttons on the camera and turns it around, my own face now on the viewfinder. At first, I don't grasp what he means—it's my face, utterly familiar. But then I catch the particular set of my jaw and the slope of my eyebrows. They're my dad's eyebrows. I haven't thought about him this much in ages and I find myself blinking rapidly.

"You all right?" Toby asks gently, removing the camera from my field of vision.

"Sure," I say, overly loudly. "It's just—you caught me by surprise with how much I look like him."

"Do you have a picture?" Toby asks. "Of your dad?"

The only one I know of in the cottage is in my bedroom. "Yeah."

"Can I see?"

It's not an odd request when this entire morning has been so surprisingly intimate.

"All right." I walk across the room and down the short hall that leads to my room in the back. I thought I'd grab the photo and bring it to Toby, but when I glance over my shoulder, he's trailing me, his amber gaze taking in everything along the way. I cautiously push open the door, but the room isn't a disaster. A few clothes thrown over the back of the green velvet armchair next to the bed, but nothing incriminating.

"This is my room," I say unnecessarily.

"Oh, you have French doors leading to your patio," Toby says excitedly. "I am so jealous. I'd love an outdoor-indoor room."

"I had them put in after I bought the place." I pick up a framed photo from the top of my big walnut dresser. It's my mother and father on their wedding day in the early '80s, with the big hair to show for it. I pass it to Toby, who looks at it with a delighted smile.

"Handsome couple. What does your mom do?"

"She's a retired teacher who substitutes part-time now. And she helps my sister with her twins."

"Twins?" Toby sounds awed. "How old?"

"Six-year-old identical boys."

"I bet they're a lot of fun and a lot of work."

"It's good they're such adorable little terrors or she and her husband might have gone off the deep end a long time ago."

"Only child here. Always thought it would be fun to be an uncle, though." He hands the photo back to me. "You do look a lot like your father."

I take one last glance before setting the picture on the dresser again. "Thanks."

It should be odd to be alone with Toby in this space, but it's not. It's comfortable, and the nervous energy I woke up with is gone, replaced by a need to spend as much time as possible with the man standing a foot away from me, to get to know him in his entirety, to have him know me. We're already off to a good start.

But I can't lie to myself about not wanting more from him, even though I accept it's hopeless. He might have called me beautiful earlier, but I know he meant it in an aesthetic, artist's eye kind of way. Even if he did mean it differently, he's off-limits. I don't mess around with guys in relationships—unless they're in an open relationship and everyone's on the same page. That could work for a brief encounter, but not for the kind of relationship the undaunted romantic corner of my heart still wants.

We clearly need to leave this room with its big comfortable bed. "Shall we go take pictures of the outside now?" I suggest.

"Sure."

"Let me put on some shoes."

Toby glances at my feet, then takes a photo of them.

"Hey, those pictures better not end up online."

He laughs. "You do have very nice feet."

Again with a compliment and a comment about my appearance. I ruthlessly shut down the tingly feeling that wants to spread from my core to my fingers and make me reach out and touch him.

"And don't worry. They will be for my eyes only," he says, while I slip on faux-shearling boots and desperately try not to read anything into his words.

"Pervert," I say affectionately as we exit through the French doors. He laughs good-naturedly and keeps taking pictures while I give him a tour of the outside, talking up a storm about the history of the house, the improvements I've made to it, the plans I have to put in a garage and a hot tub one of these days.

"The previous owners did a lot to establish the native pollinator garden," I say. "I'm no expert, but I've tried to keep it up."

"Beautiful," he says. It seems to be one of his favorite words. He touches a soft green salvia leaf. It's one of the first things that will bloom here, any day now. "I can't wait to see it later in the season."

"Come by anytime," I say. "Even if I'm not here. My friends have an open invitation."

He freezes, and I wonder if I've overstepped by implying he's a friend. But he just says, "Thanks," and starts taking pictures again.

We walk around to the front and that's where he really gets to work, eyeing the sun and ambling into the road to get some wider shots. I duck out of what I assume is the frame, but he motions me back in.

"You aren't painting me," I remind him. "Or the car."

He steps forward quickly, out of the path of an SUV that's zooming a little too fast for my liking down Bramble Street.

"True," he says. "But you are the soul of the house. I want to make sure I include the soul."

I shake my head in wonder. "I don't know how you do what you do, but I can't wait to see how this is going to turn out."

"You and me both. I know how to paint, but I can't exactly explain how it comes out looking the way it does. There's a dash of alchemy somewhere in the creative process."

"Best not examine it too closely," I advise. "And just do it."

"My thoughts exactly."

Finally, he seems satisfied with the million or so shots he's taken and comes to stand with me on the driveway between our two cars.

"Nice ride," he says. "Had her long?"

"Her?"

He winces. "It's a thing my dad does. Names all his cars. Of course, they're always female."

"So what's her name?" I ask, pointing at his station wagon.

"Helen," he says promptly.

"As in of Troy?"

"Actually, as in Frankenthaler. One of my favorite painters."

I make a mental note to look her up later. "I've never

anthropomorphized my vehicles, but if I did, this would be Daniel."

"As in?"

"Craig. Sexy and powerful—someone I'd love to take for a ride."

Toby, not put off by my innuendo, laughs. "Nice choice."

It's only after he leaves, having reminded me about Easter brunch at his and Ivy's house tomorrow, that I realize I impulsively named the car after another hot British guy I wouldn't mind getting my hands on. I hope Toby doesn't notice the parallel.

EIGHT

I'M SEEMINGLY the last to arrive at Ivy and Toby's for brunch. Jack and Pete are there, as are Van and Beck. Dulcie, an instructor at the Art Center, and her girlfriend, a musician whose name I can never remember, are here, too. Luna the cat, indifferent to the strangers coming and going from the kitchen, sits in a patch of sun smack in the middle of the floor, forcing everyone to move around her. There's an impressive array of food on the kitchen table where we ate sandwiches two weeks ago, and people are standing around talking, not quite having dived into the food yet. Ivy's in the kitchen, pouring thimblefuls of orange juice into champagne glasses full of bubbly to create the merest suggestion of mimosas.

When Toby sees me, his face lights up and he pulls me into a one-armed hug, slapping my back, and I catch a whiff of detergent smell from his collared shirt.

I don't memorize how the hug feels and push a bottle of red into his hands. "Thanks for including me." Now I've done my duty as a good guest and can duck out if I have to.

"Well, thanks for this." He glances at the bottle's label. "Would you like me to open it?"

It's a little early for a full-bodied pinot. The bottle I brought is more suited to an intimate supper in a room with dark lighting. Toby's face would still light up the darkest room. "A mimosa is fine for me," I say, nodding at his girlfriend. His *girlfriend.* God. I've got to stop this hopeless mooning.

"Ivy, Kingston will have what you're making," Toby calls over to her.

"Coming right up," she calls back.

"We're about to eat. We set up a couple of tables in the backyard since we don't really have room in the house for everyone to sit," Toby says. "By the way, I went through the photos last night and I think I got some good stuff. I'm really excited to start working on your cottage."

I pull my head out of my fantasies and into the present. "That's wonderful. How long do you think until..." I trail off when it occurs to me it's probably rude to ask when it will be finished.

Toby doesn't seem bothered. "That I don't know. At least a month, with some other things I have going on. Is that okay?"

"Of course. Take all the time you need."

A few minutes later, after a flurry of filling plates and refilling glasses, Ivy taps a fork to the side of her champagne flute. "I have an announcement to make. Pete, persistent soul that he is, has persuaded me to take a seat on the Rosedale Art Center board at the start of their fiscal year. June, is it?"

Pete nods, grinning broadly. I'm proud of him for pulling it off.

"And, in a completely unrelated coincidence, I will be mounting a show at the Childress Gallery in Queens this fall," Ivy says, smiling wider than I've ever seen her.

Congratulations abound from the guests. Toby leans over and gives Ivy a kiss on the cheek. She graciously accepts the words of praise while I pretend Toby's casually intimate gesture doesn't sour the champagne in my mouth.

"Now, find a spot to eat. There should be enough chairs for everyone, but if there aren't, you'll figure it out," Ivy says.

I top up my champagne with a liberal pour and don't bother to add more orange juice, thankful that today being a holiday gives me a reason to drink more than usual before noon. I don't regularly drink to excess, but getting buzzed might be the only way to survive this shindig. I'm the last to head outside, where I'm confronted by the sight of eight people split between two tables, four neat and tidy couples. I'm the only single one in the group and I feel like the sad uncle who's been invited out of obligation.

The self-pitying is not like me and lasts about ten seconds before I snap myself out of it and drop into the last empty chair, which happens to be between Beck and Toby.

"Beck, you really outdid yourself with the Easter egg cookies," I say. "It took all of my self-control not to fill my plate with those." Beck adapts his sugar cookie recipe for holidays and special events, making them into different shapes with intricate icing designs. His Easter eggs are large ovals with tie-dye-inspired icing in beautifully psychedelic colors and patterns. Tiny works of art in themselves.

"I confess I already stole one," Toby says sheepishly. "I have a weakness for sugar cookies."

"So do I. We've had a really busy couple of weeks in the shop with the spring holidays. Can you guess how many of these we made at the shop this week alone?" Beck asks proudly.

"Two thousand," I say.

"Four thousand," Toby guesses.

"Ten thousand," Beck says, clearly overjoyed to best us. "We had two big wholesale orders, and I had the ovens going practically twenty-four hours a day. If these whole-sale orders keep up, I might have to expand into a larger commercial kitchen space."

"That's amazing," Toby says. "You've built this business so quickly. Your cookie shop wasn't open when we moved here."

"That's the community really supporting us," Beck says. "Rosedale is such a special place."

"That I agree with," Toby says. "I've lived in cities most of my life, but they might be ruined for me after experiencing Rosedale. Small town living is like being able to take a full breath."

Beck grins at him. "I couldn't agree more. Thank goodness Jack and Pete ended up here."

I take a large sip of champagne. The bubbles burn the back of my throat. "Yet again, I get no credit for discovering Rosedale," I say, a shade harshly.

"Oh, Kingston," Beck sways out of his chair, tilting his head onto my shoulder. "You're the grandfather of all of us happy Rosedalians."

I sputter and push the youngling's head away. A minute ago I felt like the uncle; now I've been labeled a grandfather? "Thanks for that."

"What I mean is, we wouldn't be here if not for you," Beck says, laughing. "Maybe I would never have met Donovan, and fallen in love with him, and decided to open a cookie shop, and then we wouldn't be here eating Easter egg sugar cookies on a glorious April day."

"So really," Toby says, amber eyes twinkling, "we owe this gathering entirely to you, Kingston James." He raises his mimosa to me. "And we're in your debt."

"Exactly," Beck says, raising his glass as well. "To Kingston!"

"I don't know why we're toasting, but I'm always in favor of giving Kingston his flowers," Jack says from the next table over. "To Kingston!"

Now my face feels hot from the attention, and I narrow my eyes at Beck, then Toby, who looks pleased with himself. "Whatever," I grumble, uncharacteristically embarrassed. But I let the party toast me, then get back to their brunch. I may not have a partner, but it feels nice to be an appreciated member of the community, even if this toast feels goofily performative. Come to think of it, my dad would probably be pretty proud of me for influencing so many lives for the better.

And it sounds like Toby plans to stay in Rosedale for good, which means I'll have to learn to live with that.

Someday, this hard knot of longing in my chest won't hurt as much. Maybe it'll eventually fade away entirely.

I catch his eyes with mine as he bites into another cookie, crumbs clinging to his soft pink lips, before he brushes them away. He winks at me, and my entire body feels like it's on fire.

Or maybe not.

SUMMER

TOBY

NINE

I ALWAYS THOUGHT I'd have my life figured out by now.

Hilarious, right?

I'm about to turn thirty-three. And yes, from the outside I seem to have the bare minimum of functionality—I have a place to live, I have a car. I have a lovely cat and a calling. I have a girlfriend, and I have money coming in, in fits and starts, but still. I can pay my bills, when I remember to pay them.

And yet I look around and wonder what the hell I think I'm doing because in so many ways it feels like I'm treading water and there's no dock, no beach, not even a life preserver in sight.

So often it feels as if I make decisions because of what I don't want. I don't want to be like my dad. I don't want to be famous. I don't want to get a nine-to-five job. I don't want to be alone.

But lately, no matter the fact my girlfriend and I have been together for ten years, I feel oddly alone.

I thought my mom might understand. She's on the other side of the world at the moment, an anthropologist researching her latest book in Australia. She's been divorced from my dad for two decades and has been single ever since. But when I bring up my general state of confusion with her in our every-other-week phone call, she suggests I go to therapy. When I talk to my London-based therapist about it in a video call, he asks me if I'm so afraid of living my life in the negative, maybe I should try defining what I want, in the positive.

What do I want?

It scares me that the first thing that occurs to me isn't money, or success, or watching Ivy get big with our hypothetical child—something we used to talk about and haven't mentioned in at least a year. It's not even words—only a face.

Kingston James's face.

I have a secret.

I'm supposed to be working on Kingston's commission. He wanted a tidy picture of his country cottage to hang on his wall, and I started painting it—I truly did. But then I was looking through the prints of the photos I took at his house, and I kept returning to the one I took of his face, his umber skin naturally lit by the spring sunshine coming through his living room window. He was so beautiful that day. Whenever I look at that picture, that's what I see—a beautiful soul, grieving the loss of his father, striving to make it seem as if he doesn't hurt.

So I started painting something else. A portrait. Of Kingston. And I haven't been able to stop.

But wanting to paint Kingston James isn't the same as wanting him. Is it?

And the fact that Ivy hasn't touched me in months just means she's been preoccupied by getting ready for her show.

But the real red flag is that I hadn't even noticed she'd stopped touching me. Not until my therapist brings it up.

"Have you two talked about the future lately?" he asks.

"Sure," I answer automatically. "Her showing is this fall. And we're trying to figure out if we should go back to London for the holidays. I know it's only June, but if we want a good itinerary, we have to plan ahead."

"I mean the future of your relationship. Marriage? Kids?"

"We always said marriage was for other people," I answer. "You know I personally don't put much stock in the institution." Divorcing each other was the only good mutual decision my parents ever made.

"It's true you don't have to be married to be committed. But all relationships need to be worked on. They need care and attention. When was the last time you two went out together, had a date night?"

Date night? He makes it sound like we're middle-aged fogeys who need to inject some artificial romance into our lives.

But when I struggle to remember the last time the two of us did anything together, except move around each other in the kitchen while making our separate breakfasts, or discussing the day's work over dinner, I realize that since we moved to Rosedale, our comfortable cohabitation has become a situation more akin to roommates than lovers.

And I don't think a couple of date nights are going to repair a crack in our foundation that I didn't even realize was there.

I gaze at my therapist's face over thousands of miles and the two-second delay of the internet. "What if the distance between us isn't something we can fix?"

"Then you two talk about it. You decide what to do next."

The thought of Ivy not being in my life anymore makes me terribly sad. She's my best friend. But I'm starting to wake up to the fact that maybe that's not enough. That maybe there could be more for me, and more for her. And I'm holding both of us back by continuing to tread water when I could be building a boat to weather the next storm, if I'm allowed to mix metaphors.

I leave my therapy session feeling a mixture of dread and sadness. I know it's a mistake to go in and blow every-thing up, but I've been taking the tiniest baby steps for so long that if I don't take a full stride, I might as well give up.

When I bring it up to Ivy later that night, because I've always been able to talk to her about anything, the expres-sion on her face tells me more than her words. She's already been thinking about this—it's clear. It's not news to her that we've become distant. The knowledge pricks at me. Why didn't she say something?

We're sitting on the sofa in the living room, turned toward each other but with a careful two feet of space between us. Luna hops into my lap and I appreciate having something to do with my hands. I stroke her silky fur, and she settles onto my thighs.

Ivy's eyes are dry, but her mouth is sad. She tucks her legs underneath her, her oversized sweater practically drowning her torso.

"Look, Toby," she says carefully. "You chose me because I was safe. You stayed with me because you were determined not to reenact the Nathan Wheaton show, a different person on your arm every season. Well, you've proved you're not like him. And you're my best friend. But I've known for a long time that's what we've become—just friends." She plays with the bracelet on her wrist, a gold cuff speckled with flecks of clay. "You've been playing it so safe that you've hobbled yourself in life, in love, and especially in your work. I thought I was helping you by letting you take your time. But maybe I was only protecting you from making the hard choices."

"What do you mean?"

"I mean, you should be the one mounting a show in the fall. You should be displaying your work, not taking penny-ante commissions you could do in your sleep. You're a once-in-a-generation talent, Toby Wheaton, and you're hiding out in this small town."

Her vehemence startles me. "Why didn't you say something before?"

"I suppose I wanted you to figure it out on your own," she says. "I thought maybe coming to Rosedale would change things. It certainly invigorated our work. But while our art has been developing, our relationship has stagnated. And that's okay." She smiles sadly. "Some people aren't meant to be together forever."

It's sinking in that this is real. We're really breaking up. It's happened so fast my head is spinning. "But we'll—" I say, completely unable to get through the sentence without breaking down. I wipe my eyes and take a shaky breath. "We'll always be friends, right?"

She presses her lips together in a hard line, but I don't see any tears fall. "Of course, babe. We'll always be friends."

So we consciously uncouple, or whatever the ridiculous phrase is. I sleep on the sofa that night, and for the first time I realize that I'm going to have to get over myself and have a damn show, if only so I can afford a place of my own.

Growing up at thirty-three. It's not too late for me, is it?

TEN

"WOW, so you and Ivy are... over?" Pete says delicately. It's been two weeks since Ivy and I decided to change our relationship status, and Pete and I are having lunch at the Irish pub on Main Street. I'm not usually a day drinker, but the ale I'm having with my shepherd's pie seems appropriate. Pete's eating a burger and a stack of chips the size of his head.

"We are no longer together," I confirm. It hurts less to say it now—after the practice I got breaking the news to my mother and some of Ivy's and my mutual friends. Everyone's been very understanding, even encouraging, which made me think perhaps this was even longer in the making than I realized.

"Which is one of the reasons I wanted to meet up with you—I was wondering if you could recommend anywhere in town to rent. For the time being, I'm going to keep working in Ivy's garage, but I've been on the sofa for two weeks and I need my own place. Something not too expensive, though." I'm not worried about Ivy taking over the entirety of the rent when I stop paying my half. Her inheritance and her own smart investments have made money a nonissue for her. For me, not so much.

That leads me to my next huge ask, but I wait for him to respond to the first one.

"Let me think," Pete says. "You looking for a room, an apartment, or what?"

"I'd settle for a real bed on a temporary basis while I sort myself out."

"Jack and I would be happy to offer you one of our guest rooms for a while—"

"Oh, god, I didn't mean that." As I interrupt him, my cheeks feel like they're flaming. "You must think I'm a freeloader or something."

"Hey, of course not. I know how it is after a breakup," Pete says gently, because he's the kindest man on the planet. "And we really wouldn't mind. I know when I needed a place to stay after my disaster of an ex, Kingston offering me his place was a lifesaver. Wait—that's perfect."

The mention of Kingston has my face flushing for a different reason. "What's perfect?" Besides Kingston's face. And voice. And—never mind.

"Kingston's house. You could stay there. He told me he's not planning to come to Rosedale much in the first half of the summer so he can spend all of August here. So his house is completely free. I should have thought of it right away. It's been a sanctuary to more than one of us over the years."

"But I can't just invite myself to live in his home," I say, the idea of being in Kingston's space, even if he isn't there, sending me into a curious sense of longing and terror.

"I'll talk to him about it if you want."

"Oh, um." I think about it. I asked Pete for help finding a place to live and he's giving me a brilliant option if Kingston agrees. I don't actually have a good reason to turn it down, except for the vague fluttery feeling I get when I'm near Kingston, or thinking about him, or working on the portrait of him that I'm not really supposed to be working on. Besides, it sounds like he's not even going to be there, so I give myself a quick, stern talk. *Now is not the time to faff about. Now is the time to act.* "I would appreciate that. Thank you."

He seems pleased when I agree. "I'll call him later. Want some fries?"

"No, I'm okay." I take a large gulp of my ale and say the next bit while I still have my nerve. "So, the other piece of business is about work. About meeting with Fernanda Ruiz, specifically. And wondering if that's still something you think would be a good idea. I know I put you off before, but I'm trying to get my shit together and I think—I mean, I have to be, so yeah—I'm ready."

I resist the urge to hide my face in my hands. Pete isn't going to make fun of me for being useless at this. I manage to hold his gaze as he reacts to my pathetic statement.

True to form, he perks up at the prospect of being able to help. "That's great news. She has been dying to meet with you, seriously, ever since she saw your piece in the Art Center's winter show. Do you want me to give you her number? Or have her call you? Or—maybe we should all meet together?"

As much as I'd love Pete to guide me through a meeting with one of the most successful art agents in New York, I can't trespass on his kindness any more than I already have. I can do this on my own. I'm pretty sure, at least.

"I'll call her." I say. That's what new, improved Toby would do, anyway.

"There you go." My phone pings as he shares her contact info with me.

"Pete, can I ask you one more question?"

"Of course."

"Why are you being so nice to me? We're barely friends."

Pete looks surprised, and I feel bad for appearing ungrateful. He scrunches up his mouth and shrugs. "I guess I know what it feels like to be scared to take the next step in your career. When I was trying to make it happen, I made a lot of mistakes. People I trusted screwed me over."

I can all too easily imagine sweet open-hearted Pete being the target of someone's evil agenda and it makes me angry that he had to suffer.

"The art world is not for the faint of heart," he goes on. "You have what it takes to make great art that people will want to hang on their walls. But if you decided you didn't want to engage with the rest of it—well, that's your prerogative. If you do, then I want to do what I can to help you make fewer mistakes than I did. The least I can do is to get you in touch with people who aren't going to screw you over. It's called paying it forward, I think."

I reach across the table and pat his arm. "And being a

decent human being. You give us all faith in humanity, Pete."

He smiles, showing a dimple. "I've been lucky. Really lucky. And I guess I wouldn't feel right about not giving back."

"I'm lucky I met you," I say, feeling it down to my core. "And lucky we came to Rosedale."

"I feel lucky you came to Rosedale," Pete says earnestly. "And so does Jack, and the folks at the Art Center, and Kingston."

"Kingston?" His name sends a jolt of awareness through me.

"He's so excited about the painting you're doing of his house," Pete says. "I was actually going to ask you, and feel free to say no—it's not a quid pro quo thing, if you'd consider doing one for me and Jack. I know Jack would absolutely love it. But if you don't have time or don't want to, it's totally fine."

"I would be delighted," I answer, happy there's something I can do to repay his kindness. "I just need to take some reference pictures."

"Anytime you want. Thanks, Toby."

I leave lunch with Pete feeling like I've actually gained a real friend. I also have Fernanda's number and Pete's promise that he'll broach the subject of my staying at his house with Kingston.

If Kingston says yes, I'll have to confront the confusing nature of my feelings about him. But that's what grownups do, isn't it?

ELEVEN

I LET myself into my studio after my lunch with Pete, thoughts swirling around in my head so fast I close my eyes just to shut out another sensory input. I breathe in the mingled toxins of oil paint, turpentine, and lead pencils, then go to open a window. This garage-turned-studio is not climate-controlled, and while we've had a mild summer so far, the humidity levels are steadily increasing. I'll need to get a few fans out here soon.

So many paintings fill the space there's barely any room left to work. Still, I have two unfinished canvases on the easels. One is the barely started painting of the country cottage. The other has the mostly finished portrait of the cottage's owner. I remove the foam board covering that one, remembering where I left off, noting the finishing work I need to do, estimating it might be completed in another work session or two.

Why did I paint it? Because I couldn't not.

It doesn't make much sense, but that's the only explanation I have.

Ivy's car wasn't in the drive when I arrived home, and I'm surprised when she knocks on the open door of the studio while I'm still studying Kingston's portrait.

I turn to greet her without covering it up, though I selfishly want to keep him to myself for a little longer.

"Hi."

"Hi." She gives me a small smile, then shifts her attention to the painting behind me. "I didn't know you were working on portraits."

Somehow saying I've only been working on this one seems too revealing. "Um. Something new."

"It's really—" She moves closer, takes a deeper look. And then she turns to me and her eyes are full of something—regret? "It's something special."

"Thanks," I say, not sure how to interpret her mood. "Is everything okay?"

"Yeah, just wanted to tell you I'm going to the city this weekend, so you know, you'll have the house to yourself."

"I might have a lead on a place," I say. "So I could be out of here sooner rather than later."

"Really? Where?"

Saying I could soon be living at Kingston's house seems odd when his face is still dominating the room. I pull the foam board back over the canvas and pretend I didn't hear her. "I'll keep you posted."

"What about Luna?"

"What about her?"

"Can you bring her with you to your new place, or do you need me to keep her?"

I try to picture Luna stalking around Kingston's place and my heart sinks. I highly doubt he's going to want cat hair on his designer threads or his velvet armchairs. "Um, I'll get back to you."

She sighs, a bit impatiently. "Okay, well, when you have everything figured out, let me know."

"Hey, I am figuring things out, I promise."

"I'm sure you are," she says, turning around and walking out without another word.

Kingston's text comes when I'm deciding if I should get to work or find a nearby pet-friendly motel.

> Pete says you need somewhere to stay for a while. You're welcome at my place. I'm leaving for a work trip to California tomorrow, but Pete has a key, so you can let yourself in anytime. Make yourself at home. Just make sure you put the trash cans out to the curb on Tuesdays.

The offer makes me feel wholly inadequate. And yet I'm in no position to turn it down.

> I appreciate this, Kingston. One question—and feel free to say no, as she can stay with Ivy—but can I bring Luna, my cat?

There's a slight delay before he responds.

> Keep her out of my room, please. But yes. You are both my guests.

> Of course. Thank you.

I go to pack.

TWELVE

BEING in Kingston's cottage without him is odd. I've stayed in strangers' houses before, those furnished vacation rentals that make you feel like you can't actually touch anything. But Kingston isn't a stranger, even though we've only interacted a handful of times in person. We text often enough I probably could have asked him myself about staying here. But still—we're a different kind of friends than me and Pete. I'm not quite sure how to define it, except to say Pete's energy is firmly that of a friend who gets my challenges as an artist, whereas Kingston's energy draws me in and makes me want to be a part of it, somehow.

And now I have that energy all around me.

I find the guest room easily. Clean sheets are already on the comfortable bed. I brought my clothes, toiletries, all of Luna's stuff, but there wasn't much else in our house that was mine besides art Ivy and I collected together. One of these days, we'll have to split those pieces up, I suppose. Perhaps when I have a more permanent home to move to.

I make sure the door to Kingston's room is closed securely before letting Luna out of her carrier to explore the rest of the place. She sniffs the furniture, then hides under the couch. As long as she doesn't use it for a scratching post, I think we're okay.

I wander into the kitchen and put on the kettle for tea. Everything Kingston owns is good quality, well designed, and with a hint of flamboyance. His tea kettle is clear glass, his mugs all match. I recognize them as coming from the Met museum gift shop. He clearly values the items he surrounds himself with, and I feel his presence wrapping around me, even though he's three thousand miles away at his California conference by now.

Being here without him makes me miss him with a sudden, inexplicable ache.

And it's not until I'm trying to fall asleep that night in the guest bed, Luna curled up in the parenthesis of my body, that I realize it's odd that Kingston is the one I'm missing, not Ivy.

THE NEXT DAY, I screw up my courage and call Fernanda. She doesn't pick up, but I leave a message with someone who says they are "one of her assistants." How many assistants could the woman have? Then I'm back to waiting.

In the meantime, I go to the Art Center and inquire about renting studio space. I can't afford it forever, but since I'm not paying rent to Kingston, I can swing it for a while, and it's not fair to Ivy to keep taking up her space.

Unfortunately, they have a waiting list, so I put my name on it and ponder alternatives. Then I go to the grocery store because Luna needs food, and I forgot to buy it yesterday.

I get the usual assortment of produce and Luna's food, then swing by the tinned foods—beans are a reliable staple. I fill my cart with them before wandering by the fancier foods. I like a particular brand of olive tapenade they carry, and I decide to splurge and get a couple of jars. I wonder if Kingston likes olives. Before I can talk myself out of it, I locate my phone in a pocket of my jeans and text him.

> Do you like olives?

I'm deciding between boring healthy cereal and the sugary kind I still have a taste for when my phone rattles.

> Yes.

The terseness of the reply disheartens me. If my aim was to engage him in a text conversation, he's not leaving me much of an opening. I do the math—it's midmorning in California. He's probably working and I'm bothering him. I sigh. What am I even doing?

I put one of each kind of cereal in my cart and am on my way to the checkout when my phone buzzes again.

> Green are my favorite, especially stuffed with garlic. But kalamata are delicious also and those mild green ones make a tasty sauce—Castelvetranos. But you can't beat a good old-fashioned black olive. I used to put them on the tips of my fingers when I was small and pretend they were long nails like my aunties'.

> Do you like olives?

I grin and smother a laugh, then pull my cart to the side of the aisle as a grocery store employee comes through restocking.

I consider how to respond, then type.

> I love them.

> Tapenades are my favorite but I agree you can't go wrong with an old-fashioned black olive. Especially on pizza.

I bite my lip, then dare to send a follow-up.

> Be honest—did the name Castelvetranos simply roll out of your impressive brain, or did you have to look it up?

I wait, but there's no reply right away and I get nervous. Did I go too far with the impressive brain thing? Is that saying too much?

But when I'm in the checkout line, the phone buzz has me fumbling for it so fast I drop it. Thankfully, I've cracked enough phone screens in my life I now have the NASA-approved case and there's no new damage.

I read Kingston's message and tap my credit card at the same time.

> I knew it.

> But I googled it to make sure I had the spelling right.

I laugh out loud and the checkout employee gives me an odd look as they hand me my receipt.

> And now I want olive pizza. Thanks for that. I'm stuck at this conference and there's no decent food.

I wish Kingston was only as far away as his home and I could swing by Nina's and grab a pizza on the way to surprise him.

But he's in California and I'm going home to a cat.

> Maybe you could order out. When do you get back to the east coast?

> I fly to New York next Thursday. But I won't be coming to Rosedale on the weekend, if that's what you were wondering. Place is all yours for the time being.

The disappointment is swift and real. I think about how to respond as I load the groceries into the back of my wagon, then slide behind the wheel. It's warm with the late June sun coming through the windscreen, but I don't turn Helen on yet. Her air-conditioning is weak at best, anyway.

> I hope you aren't staying away on my account. I wouldn't want you to think you can't be at your own house.

I see the dots that indicate he's responding, but then they stop. I imagine him at the conference, probably being stopped by people every few minutes to talk. Perhaps he's even presenting or has some important meetings. And here I am texting him about olives.

I tell myself he wouldn't have written back if he didn't want to.

By the time I get the groceries home and inside the kitchen, the day's gotten warm enough to send me to the thermostat to check that the air-conditioner is on. Pete gave me a thorough tour of the place yesterday when he handed over his key. Hot and humid is not my preferred weather, so I hit the button to activate the air-con. A pleasantly cool draft immediately starts emanating from the floor vent in the kitchen, and I fall in love with the cottage all over again. I don't think I've ever lived somewhere with central air.

Luna winds her way around my legs, as if she knows I have treats for her in one of my shopping bags. I rip open a package of them and offer her one, because I'm not above bribing my way to love. I got her a couple of new toys, too, and I toss a hot pink feathered ball at her once she's done chewing her snack. She immediately attacks it and rolls with it into the living room. She's still a kitten at heart; I ought to spend more time playing with her. Sometimes I wish Luna had a sibling I could have adopted at the same time so they could occupy each other, but Ivy probably would have gone apoplectic.

Ivy doesn't get a vote anymore, I realize. And I get sad all over again. I guess I'm not entirely embracing this new reality. Maybe I never will fully, but I know time will help.

And work. Lots of work.

When I check my phone later, I see I've missed Kingston's reply.

> Sorry, had to duck into a meeting. And don't worry, I don't feel like I can't come home. I have engagements keeping me in the city.

I have to trust him that he's not only saying that to lessen my guilt. Still, I wonder how long it will be before I see him again. It shouldn't matter. I should be relieved that I have the place to myself for at least a few weeks. But I'm not. Maybe I'm in need of a distraction, but the idea of spending the next several weeks here alone is rather depressing.

I don't know how to tell Kingston I'd like to see him without it sounding strange.

But then he texts again.

> I'll be back for Pete's birthday barbecue. Jack said since they're going to be out of town for the Fourth, they're going to throw a big bash at the end of July. Sound good, roomie?

The end of the month? I swallow hard, but what else can I say?

Sounds good. I'll look forward to it.

He doesn't write back.

THIRTEEN

WITH THE DEADLINE of Kingston returning to Rosedale for Pete's birthday party, which I have officially been invited to by Jack via text, I have a reason to put my ass in gear and finish the painting I owe Kingston so I can move on to the one of Pete and Jack's Cape-style home. My dance card is pretty full, so I've forgotten I never heard back from Fernanda until I absent-mindedly answer a call one day after lunch and have a full-throated woman's voice in my ear.

She says she's traveling, but she'd like to see what I've been working on, and we arrange for her to come by the studio a few days after the party. I wait to panic until I'm off the phone, then I call Pete, who agrees to come over and help me curate what I have, so when she gets there I'll put my best foot forward.

In the meantime, all I can do is paint.

I'm careful to text Ivy to let her know in advance when I'll be in the studio, and she's never there when I arrive. The painting of Kingston's cottage gets finished within a week, and when it's dry enough to move, I bring it over to his place and put it in a place of honor in the living room so that Kingston will see it first thing when he gets home. I've already decided not to charge him for it—it's the least I can do after his no-questions-asked yes to letting me, and Luna, stay here.

I work on the picture of Jack and Pete's house as well. Their place is a little more polished than Kingston's, neater and more manicured, but it still has charm, and I add Cleo, their dog, which gives the thing a more personal feel. It'll be close, but I should have it done to present to them at the party.

I hold off on finishing Kingston's portrait. Something's stopping me, and I'm not sure what it is.

And Kingston and I keep texting.

At first, it's just check-ins about the house, him making sure I have everything I need.

Then I send him a picture of Luna sunning herself on his kitchen floor.

He sends me a picture of the laughably tiny fork that came with the salad he bought on the plane back to New York.

I ask him about his nephews, and he sends me some pictures of their latest antics—their mouths stained blue from ice cream truck popsicles.

> Looks like they ate a Smurf.

> EXACTLY what I told my sister.

The month zips by. I get a text from Pete the day before the party.

Just letting you know Ivy said she's
coming tomorrow.

I already knew it, since she and I talked about it when I was there working yesterday. But I appreciate the well-meaning heads-up.

Kingston texts me, too.

I'll be getting into Rosedale around
dinner time.

I rush around tidying, even though the place isn't messy, per se, just my usual stacks of magazines and doodles, plus Luna's cat toys everywhere. I make sure the fridge is stocked, and I make a run downtown to get a box of sugar cookies from Beck's cookie store. I also stop by my friend Shay's flower shop to get a bouquet of summer blooms—strong, vibrant stalks that remind me of Kingston. I set the bouquet on the kitchen table and then rethink it. It's too much.

It's not enough.

I leave it alone, come back, decide it's fine. He'll probably appreciate the gesture. Unless he's allergic to flowers. That hasn't come up in our sometimes hours-long text conversations. And now it's too late to ask. Besides, he's driving, and I don't want to distract him.

Instead, I order dinner for delivery, hoping the timing works, and go to shower off the day. It's been sticky hot all week, with frequent enough rain showers that when the heat ramps up, everything steams.

When I get out of the shower, my hair a sodden lump on my head, I hear a noise from the front room. I hope it's not Luna getting into trouble, so I pad out to scold her and perhaps corral her in my room. But instead of Luna I find Kingston, big as life, standing and staring at the painting of his cottage where I propped it on the mantel in front of the subpar watercolor he'd hung there. A Louis Vuitton overnight bag is resting on the floor by his feet and he's wearing milky coffee brown linen trousers, a linen shirt the color of freshly fallen snow. He's got a trim beard, too. That's new. How long has it been since I've seen him—two whole months?

It's only when he turns fully my way and his gaze drops approximately to my navel that I remember I'm wearing nothing but a towel. My hair drips onto my shoulders.

"Tobias Eric Wheaton," he says, uttering my full name in his big voice to great effect. Everything in me snaps to attention, my gaze sharpening on his. My nipples feel conspicuously hard in the air-conditioning, and my grip on the towel tightens.

"Kingston James," I return as smoothly as I can. "Welcome home."

He takes a step toward me, and for a moment of horrible anticipation, I think he might touch me. And if he did that, I'd embarrass myself for sure. But he doesn't reach out and I give him a crooked smile. "I thought you were Luna. I'll get dressed."

"Wait—"

I pause mid-turn.

He gestures to the painting. "It's finished."

"Yes."

"It's perfect, Toby."

I let out an invisible sigh of relief. "You like it?"

"It's lovely."

"Well, it's a lovely cottage. I've enjoyed staying here."

"I'm glad," he says warmly.

"There's—ah." Suddenly my idea of a welcome home thank you dinner feels oddly inappropriate as I stand here nearly naked, Kingston watching me with his all-knowing eyes. Texting and all the hours I've spent painting his face aside, we're still relatively new friends.

And I just got out of a relationship.

And he might not even be interested in me the way I can't seem to help but be interested in him.

And and and and...

But none of that matters. I did arrange dinner, and I owe more than a simple meal to him. Besides, I'm greedy for his attention after having to make do with scraps for so long.

Trying to sound in command, I say, "There's bubbly in the fridge, and I made cucumber water, too. If the pizza arrives, I already paid them. I'll be back in a sec."

I retreat to my room before he can demand further explanation and throw on some clothes, a pair of jeans and a black T-shirt that I'm certain I haven't worn since I washed it. I rub as much water as I can out of my hair with the towel, finger comb it away from my face, and wish I'd thought to get a haircut, but whatever. This isn't a date. It's not anything, I tell myself. It's only Kingston. The man who I haven't once fallen asleep without thinking about while lying in this bed for the past month.

Fuck me sideways.

I've built this up in my head and now I'm freaking out.

Which is stupid because as far as Kingston's concerned, I'm just the loser he's letting stay in his guest room for a while.

I swipe on some deodorant, don't bother putting on shoes or socks, and return to the living room, where Kingston's shutting the front door. He turns toward me with a pizza box in hand.

Only thing to do is brazen this out. "Great, it came. I hope you're hungry. I made a salad, too."

Avoiding meeting his gaze, I take the pizza and go to the kitchen, where Kingston must have gotten out the two glasses that sit next to the bottle of bubbly I picked up on Pete's recommendation.

"Toby?" Kingston leans against the counter and crosses his arms.

"Yeah? Do you like your salad dressed?" I put down the pizza and pick up the jar of vinaigrette I mixed together earlier. I shake it like a maraca to get the oil and vinegar to blend.

"What's all this?" Kingston doesn't sound mad or confused. Maybe a little amused.

I'm nervous, which is completely stupid, because—one more time for the cheap seats in the back—this isn't anything. "I really appreciate you giving me a roof over my head. And this is a small thank you. So, thank you."

He peers at me as if he doesn't quite believe me, but finally he says, "You're welcome." Then he opens the pizza box and lets out a sharp bark of laughter.

"Olive," he says.

"What else would it be?" I ask with a grin.

And after that, it's as easy as our text conversations.

We talk, we drink, we eat. And it's all frighteningly wonderful.

We've put away the leftover pizza and finished off the salad. "Dessert? I got sugar cookies from Beck and ice cream."

I open the freezer, and Kingston looks over my shoulder. "I'll say."

"I wasn't sure what you liked." To compensate, I basically got one of everything in the freezer aisle.

"I like..."

I wait, my hand hovering over the containers, waiting for him to finish the sentence. But he just hums. "I think I'm good, actually."

"Okay." I pull out some vanilla ice cream for myself. I pick up a spoon and a dish and take a scoop, then plop half of one of Beck's outrageous sugar cookies on top.

"Fine, I'll have some, too."

I grin and hand him that dish and make a second one for myself with the other half of the cookie.

"So, what happened with Ivy?"

The question gets tossed out there as if he's asking about tomorrow's weather and I almost choke on my bite of ice cream.

"If you don't mind my asking," Kingston adds.

"I don't mind." I'm surprised, because he never mentioned her before in any of our text exchanges. He never once asked me why I needed to move into his place. I assumed Pete filled him in.

"Pete didn't tell you?"

"He said you and she broke up, but that was it. It's none of my business, but call me curious."

"No, of course. What happened was…" I've had a lot of time to think about it, plus my weekly therapy sessions to help make sense of it in my head. "I was so scared of turning into my father that I overcorrected. She and I ran our course a long time ago, and I was too oblivious to realize it. We'll always be friends, but that's all we've been for a while. I couldn't stay there. She deserves a chance to move on properly."

"What about you?"

"I'm… working through some things. It was a bit of a rude wake-up call to realize I've been dragging my heels on truly growing up. But better late than never, right?" I try to make it sound like an opportunity rather than a burden.

"That's what they say," Kingston says neutrally.

"So, that's why this," I wave my hand around to indicate the entirety of Kingston's generosity, "has been such a life saver. I've been able to focus on the future. But you only have to say the word and I'll find someplace else to live."

"On that note, I'm planning to be here for most of August," Kingston says, and my heart sinks. He's going to throw me out. It's not that he owes me a chance, but I regret not being able to spend more time with him. "We'll really be roomies. I'm cool with it if you are."

He's not tossing me out. The relief is strong and makes me facetious. "How do you know? I could be a terrible roommate."

"You bought flowers, the place is clean, and you filled my freezer with ice cream. Even your cat is all right."

Luna's mostly kept out of our way this evening. "She's been on her best behavior, thankfully."

"And you don't have to tiptoe around me, Toby. I want you to feel at home here."

"That's not the problem," I mutter. I feel so at home I never want to leave.

"What's the problem, then?" he asks, not letting my comment slide.

I look down at my empty ice cream bowl instead of at his face. Wanting to stay, wanting to find out what his lips feel like. Those are problems. But they're not his problems, only mine. I force my gaze up to his and plaster on a grin. "No problem at all, roomie."

FOURTEEN

IN THE MORNING, I feel oddly self-conscious as I go about the routine I've developed since moving here. It's different knowing Kingston—my host... my *friend*—is only a wall away. But I can't hide out in my room all day. Besides, Jack and Pete's barbecue is today and I'm going to give them their painting.

I let Luna out of my bedroom first, then join her in the kitchen where I pour her some breakfast before tending to my own needs. It doesn't seem like Kingston has been up yet. Is he a late riser? We didn't overdo it last night, but maybe he's avoiding me.

I have eggs frying and am wrangling hot toast when he appears, shuffling from the direction of his room, scratching his beard and peering at me with bleary brown eyes.

He's wearing old-fashioned blue and white striped pajama pants and nothing else. I've never seen him in so little before and my gaze skims his smooth, almost hairless chest and belly, then lower, noting the way the material folds and hangs over the bulge between his legs.

My eyes snap upward and my, "Good morning," doesn't come out too strangled.

"Morning," he says, voice rough. "Too early."

"Did I wake you? Sorry, I—"

"No, I was up. Need to be up." He reaches for the kettle. "Party today, right?"

"Yes."

"You want to head over together?" Kingston asks casually and I relax. God, it's like I don't know how to be normal anymore.

"I have to go by my—Ivy's. To get something for Pete and Jack."

"You did a painting of their house, too, didn't you?"

I nod. "It's a surprise that it's arriving today, though."

"I'll keep my lips sealed."

"Anyway, it's done, but the paint is still tacky. I wouldn't want to risk Daniel's upholstery." And I don't want him to accidentally see the portrait. I'm not sure how he'd react.

"All right. Meet you there, then."

It's more distracting than it should be to navigate around a shirtless Kingston in his kitchen, but why shouldn't he be allowed to be comfortable in his own space? Besides, I'm the one who greeted him in a towel yesterday evening. I suppose it's all part of cohabitating with someone I happen to find incredibly attractive.

I settle into my usual spot at the bar with my eggs and toast, while Kingston heads to the fridge and pulls out the remnants of last night's pizza.

He's usually so fastidious that I'm completely shocked when he pulls a piece out and starts eating it standing up next to the fridge. "What are you doing?"

He stares at me. "Eating breakfast?"

"But you're Kingston James. I never thought I'd see Kingston James eating cold pizza for breakfast."

"Cold pizza for breakfast is the best way to eat pizza," he says, his eyebrows all crooked as if he thinks I'm the weird one.

"Guess I don't know you as well as I thought I did."

"Guess you don't," he returns easily. "I'm not just a fussy know-it-all with impeccable taste. I'm a fussy know-it-all with impeccable taste who likes cold pizza for breakfast."

I laugh and bite into my eggs, sending yolk running down my chin. Kingston wrinkles his nose and grabs a napkin from the counter, reaches forward and swipes it across my face.

His thumb catches on my cheek before he drops the napkin into my hand.

"And you are a mess," he says evenly.

I clean myself up, feeling silly for the way his touch makes my heart kick up.

I definitely have a crush on him.

But we're living together.

It's complicated.

And I ought to be focused on my career. That's the point of all of this, anyway. Moving out. Moving on.

So I forget about what seeing him in nothing but thin pajama pants does to me. I forget about how all I want now that he's back is to spend time with him. I harden my shell, clean up my dishes, scratch Luna behind the ears.

"See you at the party," I say.

"See you there."

FIFTEEN

JACK AND PETE have a huge backyard, with a big green lawn that extends to the ring of trees that demarcates their property, a big flagstone patio that has a table and chairs and a grill the size of my first flat, and even a pool, hidden behind a gate off to the side. When I arrive, toting my gift, the patio is already littered with people. Some of them I know, like Shay and his boyfriend Connor, who happens to be Luna's vet's son. I also see Van and Beck, who are playing with Jack and Pete's dog, Cleo. I recognize some people from the Art Center—Dulcie and Che and a few others. And there's Ivy, looking as polished as ever in a jade green off-the-shoulder sweater and a cream skirt, talking with an athletic-looking man who's gesticulating with his hands. I set the painting down in a safe corner, face tilted toward the wall to keep the contents private, and head to Ivy first, since I don't see our hosts. Kingston doesn't seem to have arrived yet, either.

"More bike parking is really essential," the athletic man is saying when I walk up.

"Oh absolutely," Ivy agrees, "but who's going to pay for it?"

"I was thinking we could get local businesses to under-write the costs in exchange for signage. You know, like 'this bike rack provided by Wine and Roses,' sort of thing," he says.

"I love it. Hello, Toby," Ivy says smoothly. "Do you know Charlie?"

The man offers me a hand. "Charlie Linden."

"Toby Wheaton," I reply. The name jogs my memory. This is a good friend of Jack's. "You just opened the bike shop, right?"

"I did," he says. Fixing me with a keen eye, he asks, "Do you ride?"

"Ah—not as such," I say, feeling inadequate. "But maybe I should get into it?"

I trade a glance with Ivy, who looks entertained. A fellow with messy dark hair comes up and stands next to Charlie. "Are you proselytizing again?" he asks, the fond note in his voice taking away the sting.

"We were talking about the shocking lack of bike parking in downtown Rosedale," Charlie says a hair defen-sively. "But we can talk about something else. Drew, this is Ivy Miller; she just joined the Art Center board. And this is Toby."

I wave at Drew, who I've never met but know of from conversations with Jack and Pete. "I loved *Dessert First*. Great film."

"You work in the movies?" Ivy asks.

"Film editor," Drew says.

"That is fascinating." I knew Ivy would be intrigued.

She quickly pulls Drew away and starts peppering him with questions.

It's odd to be here with her, but not *with* her. It doesn't feel awkward, but it doesn't feel normal, either.

"You should come into the shop sometime. I could get you fixed up with a starter bike."

I tune back into Charlie. "Uh, maybe when I'm a bit more stable. I'm living in a friend's guest room for the time being and I already brought in a cat. I don't think I can add a bike to the mix just now."

"Fair enough. We have a cat," Charlie says, nodding at Drew, who seems to be answering Ivy's questions graciously. "But we're thinking about getting a dog, too."

"Dogs are a lot of work. I grew up with one." Darwin was a high-maintenance poodle that I remember causing a lot of arguments between my parents when they were still together. Looking back, maybe Mom was more pissed about Dad running around on her with other women than about the fact he'd forget to take Darwin for walks when Mom was busy getting her Ph.D. "Cats are much easier."

"But you can't take them for a run," Charlie counters.

"You could try. I knew a girl in London who took her cat about on a lead. Not sure if the cat really enjoyed it, though."

"Cinnamon would never," Charlie says. "So, what do you do?"

"I'm a painter."

Charlie's interest sharpens. "Really? Drew and I have been looking for someone to do our house."

I'm taken aback by the coincidence. "That seems to be

the theme of the summer," I say. "I just did Jack and Pete's."

Now Charlie looks confused. "I didn't know they'd had their house painted recently."

"I haven't shown it to them yet," I say as Pete and Jack come out on the patio, each carrying a large platter of food. "In fact, I better take care of that now."

I leave Charlie behind, tap Pete on the shoulder after he sets a tray of watermelon slices onto the table. "Happy birthday, man," I say. "And I have something for both of you." Jack joins us, looking excited as a puppy eyeing a tennis ball when I retrieve the painting.

I flip it so the picture faces out, to legitimate oohs and aahs from the nearby guests. "I hope you like it." It's a sincere statement and not a plea for compliments.

Pete and Jack just stare at it in silence, glance at each other in unison, then both burst out talking at the same time, so fast that I can barely keep up.

"Incredible, gorgeous. Do you see the light in the trees?"

"I can't believe how pretty it is. Babe, it's our home."

"And is that Cleo? It's Cleo!"

"Cleo. God. Toby. It's amazing. Thank you."

I let myself relax. They like it. Pete puts his hands out and I transfer the painting to his care. "You're welcome, guys. You've been so kind to me, both of you."

"It's such a lovely memento," Jack says.

"Wait 'til you see mine." Kingston's suddenly there. When did he arrive? I smile at him and he smiles back. The party suddenly seems much more enjoyable. "But yours is nice, too."

"So you're like a painter, painter," Charlie says, his face oddly red.

"Yes?" I respond uncertainly.

"I thought you meant house painter, not painter of houses," he says, sounding embarrassed.

"Oh! That's my bad. Maybe I should have said artist?"

"You're definitely that," Charlie says, looking more closely at the painting in Pete's big hands. "That's impressive."

"I like painting houses that have souls."

"Then you actually do have to paint our house," Charlie says. "It's this old farmhouse, and it has soul up to the chimney. But maybe wait until we actually get the outside painted by an actual house painter."

"I can give you a name for that, Charlie," Pete says.

"But maybe I should take pictures of it the way it is now," I suggest. "The painting might be more interesting if the subject is less polished."

"Whatever you think is best. Wow, this is really cool. So this is your deal—you paint houses?"

"Among other things," I say.

"By the way, I'm free tomorrow," Pete says to me. "Early afternoon?"

My gut lurches when I realize he's talking about the curation we need to do to prepare for Fernanda's visit to my studio. "Okay, thanks."

"Now, where should I put this masterpiece?" he says. "I want everyone to be able to see it."

"It's still a little wet," I caution. "I'd put it out of reach, especially of the animals."

Pete takes the painting inside to find it a safe home,

and Jack gives me an unexpected hug, then leaves his hand on my shoulder so he can look into my eyes with his green ones. "It's perfect. Thank you, Toby."

"You're welcome." In my peripheral vision, I catch Kingston looking at us with a funny expression on his face. "Thanks again. Pete's been a rock for me this summer."

"He's been where you're at," Jack says. "It's all good. The world needs your art."

I laugh. "I think I read that on a bumper sticker."

"Doesn't make it not true," Jack says, unoffended by my flip remark. He turns to fuss over the buffet. "Time to eat, people!"

"Sounds like you have another commission in the works," Kingston says.

"Maybe," I say. "I'll run out of Rosedale houses, eventually."

"You're going to be too big for Rosedale soon enough," he says.

"What do you mean?"

"Once Fernanda sets you up with your big New York show, it's all over for us. You'll be hot shit, and we'll say, 'We knew him when.'"

I laugh uncomfortably. "She's only coming to look—no promises."

"But you do want to have a show, don't you?" he presses. "Get your work out there more."

I sigh and cross my arms over my chest, feeling defensive even though I know he's asking the right question. "I know I should, but it's complicated. Right now I feel like I'm holding on so tight to my paintings they're going to crumble in my hands. And that's not what I want, either."

"You're doing the right thing by meeting with Fernanda. Sometimes to grow, things have to get scary."

"Yeah—what scary things have you been up to?" It's easier to turn things around on him than contemplate the terror that is exposing my work to the vicious tongues of the art world.

"Actually, I'm working on opening my own agency. It's scary as hell." He doesn't sound scared, though. He sounds excited, in control. What I wouldn't give for a fraction of his confidence.

"Wow! I had no idea. It sounds like a big undertaking."

"It's one of the reasons I've been in the city so much. I'm wooing a couple of agents who I want to set up shop with. We'll pool our resources and make something new. I want a shop where agents don't have to be worried they won't make their mortgage payments if they don't sell something that month. Everyone gets a guaranteed base salary and benefits."

"That's remarkable. And not usually how it works, is it?"

"It's not an entirely new idea, but it's risky. But I've been successful enough to be able to put plenty aside for a cushion. Hopefully, I'll be able to nurture some new talent this way."

Of course he wants to use his success to mentor others. "That's so exciting, Kingston."

"And scary," he adds with a smile. "Suddenly I'm going to have all these people depending on me. But if it works, it'll make things better for everyone."

"I love that. And I have no doubt it'll work. What's the next step?"

"Well, publishing gets quiet in August, so I'm taking some time off to recharge, then in the fall it'll be full steam ahead. Lawyers and LLCs and looking for office space."

"Office space? In New York?"

"Where else?"

It is the center of publishing. Makes sense that Kingston would make it his home base. I'm just greedy for wanting him around more. Not that we'll still be roommates by the fall. I should find someplace else to live by then.

"Kingston, hey." Ivy walks up to us and greets him with a kiss on the cheek that makes me unaccountably grumpy. "I haven't had a chance to thank you for giving this one a roof."

"My pleasure, darling," he drawls. "How've you been?"

I excuse myself, for some reason, not wanting to hear them make small talk. I get some food, pour myself a tall glass of iced tea, and sit down next to Van Eastman. I was intimidated by the handsome, somewhat aloof actor the first couple of times I met him, but the more we talked, the more I got that he's actually a softie, especially when he's around his boyfriend, Beck. Something about the blond baker makes Van softer, more approachable.

I take a bite of pasta salad and watch Kingston and Ivy from afar. They seem to be deep in a conversation that apparently requires Ivy to touch Kingston's arm every three seconds.

"Something wrong with the pasta salad?" Van asks worriedly. "It's not off, is it?"

"Off?" I look down at my fork, then back at Kingston and Ivy. "No, it's delicious."

"You looked like you had a bad taste in your mouth." He follows the direction of my gaze and hums thoughtfully. "I heard about you and Ivy. Are you okay?"

"Sure. I'm getting there." Ivy puts her hand on Kingston's shoulder and they both let out peals of laughter that I can hear across the yard. My grip on my fork tightens. What is going on with me? Ivy is a gorgeous woman, but I was never jealous over her. I'm not even with Kingston, but I feel some kind of way about him being touched by other people, including my ex—which is absurd.

Abruptly, I put down my fork and flash Van a weak smile. "Sorry. Distracted." It's not like Kingston would be interested in her, anyway. From everything I've picked up about him from his friends and his own words, Kingston's gay.

But what if I've missed something? I look around, see that Van and I are relatively isolated. "Forgive me for the question, but Kingston's gay, right?"

"Oh, yeah," Van says in a knowing voice. I narrow my eyes at him.

"What? We were all young once," he says. "Kingston and Pete and I have known each other forever."

"Kingston and Pete—" The thought had never occurred to me before, but it's not impossible that they could have been together at one point, though Pete's obviously devoted to his husband now.

"No, I don't think so. Just friends."

I can't help an audible sigh of relief. Something about

picturing Kingston with anyone else makes my intestines feel like they're tied in knots.

"So Beck was right," Van murmurs lowly. "He swore you weren't straight."

I've been the topic of their speculation? That's enough to take my attention off Kingston and Ivy to fully focus on Van. "I'm bi." It seems important to be clear. "Always have been."

"Awesome," he says easily. "But you need to be careful if you're thinking about hooking up with Kingston."

I cough on my sip of iced tea, and it takes a moment before I can get a word out. "I'm not—Kingston and I are friends. He's giving me a place to live. We're just friends." The denials come out as fast as I can make my tongue move.

Van's blue eyes soften in something like sympathy. "Kingston is the most together person I know. He's also one of the best men I know. But he hasn't always had the best luck in love. And I like you, Toby, but it's my job to watch out for him, if you get my drift?"

"Of course. But—" I'm about to deny everything when out of the corner of my eye I catch Kingston's profile as he browses the buffet. I think about how we'll go home to the same house, how he'll be only a few rooms away for the next several weeks. He and I really are becoming friends, and this time is supposed to be about work for me. I can't afford to destabilize my life even more right now. And Kingston doesn't deserve to have even more of my chaos foisted on him.

Van's right—I'm borrowing trouble. But I can't help it.

Kingston's in my head and I don't know how to get him out. The best I can do is keep my feelings to myself.

I offer Van what I can. "I'll be careful."

He slaps my back. "Good man."

Kingston appears at our table like a jump scare. "What are we talking about?" he asks, elegantly settling into the chair to my right.

I freeze, then take a big bite of pasta salad to avoid having to answer.

Van smoothly steps in. "Did you know Beck and I got a dog?"

"Mazel tov," Kingston says. "Tell me more."

"Her name is Molly, and she's a sweetheart. We're still getting used to each other, but so far so good."

I tune them out while they talk about Molly's many fine qualities. Kingston and I are friends, roommates. No matter how my feelings for him seem to grow by the minute, I'm going to keep them locked down.

SIXTEEN

PETE MEETS me at Ivy's garage the next day. We put on some music and start sorting through the scores of paintings I've amassed over the past few years. I had what I thought was my best work shipped from England when we moved here, but I've barely looked at it since then. It's strange to study those pieces now. I see the technical proficiency in them, but there's also something different about them from the pieces I've worked on in the States; a different feel, a different energy. Almost like they were painted by someone else.

Pete has a good eye, and he's not emotionally attached the way I am, so he combs through the canvases faster, indicating two general types he thinks we should present to Fernanda—my English coastal landscapes and my New England architectural paintings.

"What's that?" he asks, pointing to the canvas on the easel with the foam board covering it.

"Oh. Well. Something new." I bite my bottom lip.

"Can I see?"

I can't think of any sensible reason why he shouldn't.

"It's not quite finished," I warn. I don't know why I haven't been able to complete it. I pull the cover away.

Kingston's face looks back at us, three times life-size. Today the set of his lips seems knowing instead of contemplative.

Pete makes an aborted sound, then takes a couple of steps back from the painting. "It's... not what I was expecting," he says, glancing at me quickly. "Not that I was expecting anything. But wow, it's—you have to show this to Fernanda, Toby."

"Why? I don't have anything else like it."

"For one thing, it's gorgeous." Now he steps closer to the painting and peers intensely. "You know the way you have of making your buildings look more real than real? You've done the same magic trick with this. It's Kingston, a Kingston that looks so real he could start talking to us. But it's not a photograph. It's remarkable."

"I used some photos as a reference." I show him the stack of them on the workbench. "I was just, I don't know, taken up by it."

"You haven't done any other portraits?"

"I have, over the years." I try to make it sound like it's not a big deal, as if I tossed this one off in an afternoon, instead of being consumed by it for weeks. "But not lately. Just this one."

I wonder if he can hear what I'm not saying. Just Kingston.

As if a handful of puzzle pieces all click together in his head at once, he swivels his neck quickly, like a bird, and eyes me steadily.

"Toby."

"Pete."

"Are you and Kingston—is that why you and Ivy—not that it's any of my business, it's just Kingston is one of my oldest friends and—"

I rush to reassure him. "No, and no, and Van gave me this speech yesterday. Kingston and I are friends," I say firmly. "And roommates, at the moment. And he has nothing to do with Ivy and me splitting up. That was a long time coming."

He looks relieved, and I feel slightly disingenuous, but all of this is true. Yesterday, I vowed to put away those inconvenient feelings for Kingston. I'm trying my best.

We move on, finish sorting out the paintings, and I put the ones I won't show Fernanda together in the corner.

"Nice of Ivy to let you keep this place," Pete says while we tidy up.

"She's a nice woman," I say. "But I have been trying to find somewhere else. The Art Center doesn't have any free studio space just now."

"Hmmm. Let me think on it," Pete says.

"You know, you don't have to solve everyone's problems for them," I say. "You've already done so much for me."

"What are friends for?" Pete says it so unironically that I have to laugh. "What?" he asks.

"You're an odd duck, Pete. Most of the people I've met in the art world with your level of success are egotistical jerks, competitive and cutthroat. But you put your hand out to pull me up like it's nothing."

"You know I was burned," he says simply, not

sounding sorry for himself, or even angry. "And it took the support of Jack and Kingston and my friends at the Art Center and eventually Fernanda to not only put my art front and center again, but to really heal from those burns. I came to Rosedale to hide, to heal, but it didn't really work until I let people help me. I guess I see myself in you, trying to do it on your own so hard you're holding yourself back. But it's not cheating to make friends, to make connections. That's being part of a community. And if you never want to join that community and step outside of Rosedale, well, that's fine. But I truly think you can handle it out there in the big, bad art world."

"That's quite a declaration," I say, trying to stay professional and not break down at the simple kindness of being included in the community he's describing.

"Accepting help isn't the same as using people," Pete says. "Believe me, I know the difference."

"Thank you," is all I can think to say.

And by Pete's answering smile, I know that's all he needs to hear.

I'M nervous the next morning getting ready for Fernanda's visit. She's taking the train in, and Pete's going to pick her up at the Rosedale station. He'll bring her directly to the studio and then we're all going to the Greystone Inn's dining room for a fancy lunch that I'll have to put on a credit card but have already decided I absolutely cannot allow Pete to pay for.

"What is going on in there?" Kingston asks, knocking on my door. "It sounds like you're tearing down a wall."

"No." I yank open the door and gesture to my bed, which has every article of clothing I own on it, except the baggy gray shirt and dark green boxers I'm currently wearing. The boxers I had on to sleep in—even with the air-con it's been too warm to go to bed in much beyond underwear, especially with the heat generated by my feline companion. "I'm having a really hard time deciding what to wear and I got my suitcase down from the top of the closet to see if I had magically forgotten some perfect outfit in there and I dropped it."

"What, you can't decide between which black sweater and which pair of paint-covered jeans?" he deadpans.

"Kingston, not helping," I wail.

He chuckles. "I don't think it really matters. You're an artist. Artists are always given a pass on their clothes. You could wear a traffic guard vest and she'd think you were making a statement."

"But I don't have a traffic guard vest," I say. "I have wrinkled T-shirts."

"Hey, it's going to be okay," he says, his voice soothing. "This isn't about clothes, is it?"

"It is partly," I say mulishly.

"It's going to go fine. I've met Fernanda, and she's actually just a regular human being, you know."

"She's an art agent," I correct. "A powerful one."

"Not a space alien," he says firmly. "Now, how about these?" He goes to my bed and holds up my one pair of black jeans.

"Aren't skinny jeans out?"

He rolls his eyes. "Now you care about fashion?"

"Fine." I snatch the jeans from him. "What else?"

"Don't you have a blazer somewhere?"

"It's too hot." I know I shouldn't be complaining; my nerves are definitely getting the better of me.

"Hang on." He disappears.

I've changed into clean underwear and the black jeans by the time he comes back holding three items on identical soft gray hangers.

He holds up a dress shirt in some thin material, a busy pattern of bright flowers that's much more his style than mine, if I can claim to have any style at all. He shakes his head and switches it to the back of the options before I can even veto it. Then he lifts a T-shirt, plain white with a reproduction of an Andy Warhol lithograph on it. He keeps his T-shirts on hangers?

He misreads my expression and asks, "Too on the nose?"

"Too big—Kingston, your clothes aren't going to fit me."

"Why not? We're practically the same height."

I stare at him. "You can't be serious. Your shoulders are like twice the breadth of mine."

The other morning, when he came into the kitchen in only his pajama pants, I couldn't help noticing that those shoulders, always hidden behind his carefully curated layers, were surprisingly powerful, his chest not bulging with muscle but more developed than my own thin frame. He has one of those inverted triangle builds that if I were a sculptor, I'd love to try to capture in marble. Perfect proportions and miles of smooth skin to run my hands over.

But I'm not a sculptor. And I've already trespassed against him by painting his portrait without permission.

"I think you're underestimating yourself, or overestimating me," he says casually. "Just try it, with this." He hands me the last of his finds—a lightweight linen jacket, white as a narcissus flower. When I slip it off the hanger, I notice the store's tag is still pinned to the sleeve and glimpse the price.

"You spent six hundred dollars on this? And you've never worn it?" I hastily try to shove it back into Kingston's hands, but he laughs.

"It was on sale. I think. And I was saving it for a special occasion. It turns out I was saving it for *your* special occasion. Try it on. Please?"

Since I owe him way more than that, I nod and shut up. Off goes the gray shirt, on goes the Andy Warhol. It's a little baggy, but when I slide the jacket on top, I don't think anyone will be able to tell. The jacket itself feels like butter against my arms, and when I look in the mirror, I see someone hip and fashionable staring back.

I close my eyes. I'm such a fraud.

"What—you don't like it? Because you look amazing," Kingston says easily.

"No, it's great." I open my eyes. "Thanks for your help. You could have a second career as a stylist. I just—I'm not scared she's not going to like my stuff. I'm scared she *will* like it. What if I'm not ready, not good enough, for what comes next?"

He comes up to me, and for a second I think he's

reaching for my hand, which causes my heart to speed up in surprise—in hope?—but he's actually reaching for the tag. He carefully unhooks the microscopic safety pin holding the tag to the inner seam without touching me.

"Toby, take it one step at a time. You won't know if you can handle it until you're doing it. But you'll never find out until you take that step. And I think you're ready. Pete does, too. And if you need help, you've got it. We'll be there for you, all right?"

He waits for me to nod. From this close I can see the swirling browns in his eyes, the individual hairs in his tidy new beard. It frames his full lips and all I'd have to do to feel them against mine would be to lean forward.

But that would be taking much more than I've been given, and so much more than I deserve.

"Thanks, Kingston," I whisper. Louder, I add, "I'm ready." I might not entirely believe it, but I owe it to him to pretend that I do.

SEVENTEEN

"GOD IT'S HOT. I thought the city was disgustingly humid, but at least there's air-conditioning." Fernanda Ruiz isn't taciturn. A tall woman in her late fifties with unnaturally black hair and a city-chic pantsuit that looks faintly silly in casual country Rosedale, she hasn't stopped talking since she and Pete arrived at Ivy's. She waves a hand in front of her face, and I'm glad I thought to put a couple of fans in the studio this morning. It is hot—I'm sweating through Kingston's shirt and feel glad to have the protection of the jacket. Ivy is here, too—Fernanda's the one who put her in touch with the gallery where her show is going up in a few weeks and she wanted to meet her in person. Everyone is all smiles, and I try to pretend this is simply a no-stakes studio visit.

"Everyone is talking about your show, darling," she says to Ivy while we walk from the house to the garage. "Who's doing your PR?"

"I'm talking to someone from Rosenblum Associates," Ivy says, which is news to me. I'm not surprised she's on top of this—Ivy's always been better at the business stuff. Fernanda shares her approval, then Ivy says, "Well, I'll let you three have some privacy," giving me an encouraging nod before she turns back to the house.

Pete, thank everything that is holy for the man, leads the tour through my art. I try not to seem like a weirdo, hovering awkwardly while other people discuss my work, almost as if I'm not here. They go through the seaside landscapes first, and Fernanda makes many exclamations of adoration, which I can't tell are put-ons or not. She sounds more organically enthusiastic about my New England architectural paintings.

"Very nice. Is that a dog? People love animals. That's why Ivy's hummingbirds and horses are going to sell out," she says definitively, as if saying it will make it so.

I smile at her weakly.

Abruptly, she points. "What's that?"

At Pete's suggestion, I've left Kingston's portrait on the easel, but covered.

I walk over and take the foam board away. "It's something new. Not quite finished," I say, trying not to sound apologetic.

Fernanda comes close, settling rhinestone-studded glasses on her nose. "Wait, I know this face. The book agent, Kingston Josephs, am I right?"

"Kingston James," I correct. "It's different, I know."

She hums, then looks at it for a full minute in absolute silence.

I glance at Pete and raise my eyebrows in question, but he just shrugs.

"Do you have more portraits?" she asks.

"Not really. It's a bit of a one-off."

She hums again, and stares at it without speaking. The only sound is the whir of fans chopping up the close air.

I feel like I might go crazy if someone doesn't say something, but then Fernanda straightens and turns around, whipping off her glasses and tucking them into her designer handbag.

"Well, shall we go to lunch?" she asks brightly.

That's it? We've only been here for fifteen minutes. "Um. All right."

Does this mean I've blown it? No agent? No future? I'm surprised at the strength of my disappointment. I thought I'd be fine with staying under the radar, painting the houses of my friends for small commissions. But I suppose my ego's been biding its time all along.

"Do you want to take any pictures?" Pete asks, trying to salvage something of the encounter.

"No, I'll leave that task to Galia and Grayson. I'll have them come up and catalog everything. I'll give Galia your number, Toby, and you can tell her when it's convenient. But let's get this done before Labor Day. There's a hole in the Weiss Gallery's March schedule and I think we can slot you in there. Normally you'd have to wait eighteen months for them, but the star of their spring show went to rehab and came out utterly unable to paint. Which is good for you, darling."

I wince at the callous mention of the poor anonymous painter whose misfortune is apparently my gain. And am I supposed to know who Galia and Grayson are? "So, you want to represent me?"

"Oh, my, yes, didn't I say that? You know you're

talented—but more—you're sellable. Modern, but classic. Approachable, but flawless technique. In other words, eminently marketable, darling. A real find. Pete—I owe you a boon for bringing me this lovely boy."

"I'll keep that in mind," Pete says, a satisfied smile on his face.

I'm glad he seems happy, but my head is still spinning. "So, that's it?"

"We'll sign a contract, of course. And you—you need to paint more of those." She points directly at Kingston's face. "I want to see more portraits. Do this one, while you're at it," she swings her pointer finger to Pete, "and anyone else you can find to sit for you."

"I usually work from photographs."

"Even better," she booms. "More portraits," she repeats. "Let's see, we'll stage the show in February, open early March. That gives you months of production. And plenty of time to line up some press, though magazines might be tricky. But let's see if we can squeeze in some portraits alongside your quaint houses. People like looking at beautiful people, don't they? It'll draw them in."

I must have some kind of frozen look on my face, because she taps me on the shoulder as if she wants the attention of a wandering child. "You can do more portraits, can't you? You're a working artist. You can paint what you need to paint." She says it like it's not a question, and on this, I agree. I've never been the sort of artist who necessarily needs to be in the mood to paint. Working every day, whether I feel like it or not, is what's gotten me to this point. Kingston's portrait was an aberration—I couldn't have stopped painting that one if I'd been handcuffed and could only hold a brush between my teeth. But normally I head to the studio like it's an office, put in the hours, and do the work.

"Yes," I agree firmly. "That I can do."

"Good boy," she says. "Toby, your life is about to change. You're going to be very successful and you're going to make more money in a month than you've probably seen in your life. It's all going to be very magical and confusing. But you have me and Pete and Ivy and your boyfriend Kingston to help you. Now, let's go have lunch."

My mouth feels numb and I follow them to Pete's car on autopilot. She's going to represent me. My life already feels like it's changing. And it's so overwhelming I don't think to correct her about Kingston being my boyfriend. It's not until much later that I wonder where she got that idea in the first place.

FALL

KINGSTON

EIGHTEEN

MY AUGUST VACATION went by too fast, and going back to the city in September gave me back-to-school vibes. I saw less of Toby while I was chilling in Rosedale than I thought I might—once he signed the contract with Fernanda and the date of his show in New York was set for March he was suddenly in a frantic race to prepare. Seven months away sounds like a lot, but I work on a publishing calendar where seven months are merely a couple of blinks of an eye.

He's working on new paintings, I know, but he won't say what. We developed a routine over the summer, sharing the kitchen during breakfast hours, then he'd go to his studio at Ivy's house, and I'd lounge around and read before heading to Pete and Jack's to use their pool. In the afternoons, I would get some work done, keeping up with my clients and their projects, and moving forward on my plans for my agency.

I'm aiming to officially open January 1, which feels both so far away and like no time at all.

And I've mostly kept my feelings for Toby under wraps. I assumed living with the man would be the perfect chance to get up close and personal with his annoying habits and off-putting tendencies, which would aid me in getting over my inconvenient crush. Only problem—he doesn't seem to have any flaws, unless you count doting on his cat. And the fact that he sees his ex-girlfriend of a decade all the freaking time. Am I jealous? I have no right to be anything when it comes to Toby. We're friends, though, for sure now, and that's not bad.

So I've been irrevocably ruined by seeing him shirtless more times than I can count. So he smells way too good for a man who spends his days around mildly toxic chemicals and barely remembers to do laundry. So his sleepy early morning smile makes my heart flip, and the way we stand next to each other in my kitchen and wash up after dinner together, talking about movies and art and books and our childhoods, makes me constantly wish that we were going to share the same bedroom after finishing up instead of going to our separate ones—

Other than that, I've got my feelings on complete lockdown.

Right.

But now that I'm back to my regular routine in the city, I miss him more than I should. My apartment seems so empty and dull compared to the colors and the noise of the house Toby and I share.

I even miss the cat.

Work is good, at least. Three of my top choices were successfully wooed and all say they're on board with the Kingston James Literary Agency. All I have to do is finalize the paperwork, find the perfect office space, and pull the trigger.

Easy peasy.

EARLY OCTOBER and it's finally starting to feel like fall in the city, after a late-summer heatwave that kept us inside and out of the humidity. But today the air has a chilly snap to it and the trees in Central Park are getting with the program and donning their autumnal colors. I usually take the subway to the office, but today I walk, wanting to feel the cooler air and think. About Toby—big surprise.

He's been at my place for over three months and so far he hasn't mentioned finding anywhere else to live. I've never had a roommate for so long—usually when I offer to host people it's for a few weeks, and I'm normally only there on weekends. This thing with Toby has been the most permanent cohabitation situation I've had since college, but I find myself anxious when I think about him moving out. The only rub is his workspace. He's still going over to Ivy's to paint since he hasn't been able to find another space in Rosedale.

The relationship he has with Ivy is... confusing. Not that I don't know plenty of exes who stayed friends with each other, but they seem closer than most.

Am I jealous—of course. Am I still reeling that they broke up at all—also yes. They seemed so comfortable with each other, like an old married couple. But perhaps that was the problem, or at least that's what I gathered from the times Pete and Toby himself talked about it. I can relate—Sergio and I were like that, better as friends, not enough spark to keep things going. Sad, but it happens.

But in the last few months, I've had to remind myself more than once that just because he's not with Ivy anymore, it doesn't exactly make him available. And it definitely doesn't make him interested in me.

I know he values our friendship. I know he appreciates having a place to live. But beyond that, thinking anything else could happen is asking for heartache.

> I'm in town through Friday—want to get a drink?

I read the text before looking at the sender and my heart jumps at the idea that Toby could be in New York. He'd mentioned that he would probably be coming here to meet with the gallery curator in charge of mounting his show. Then I see the text is from Van, which makes more sense. Van's home base is now Rosedale, but he's frequently in the city, what with his acting jobs, auditions, and lately fine-tuning the play he wrote that's in workshop.

I check my schedule and write back.

> I'm meeting an editor for dinner tonight. Want to meet me at Da Capo after?

> Definitely. See you there.

My meeting goes well—it looks like my client Reed Bennet's first YA novel will find a home with our top choice of publishing houses—so I'm in a great mood when

I arrive at Da Capo. Van's already there at a two-person table in a dark corner. He's nursing a beer, so I order a glass of wine on my way over.

We exchange a hug, and I shed my London Fog overcoat. "I haven't seen you since you and Beck got engaged. Congratulations, again, in person."

He smiles, wide and open, and I can't believe how he's changed since he met Beck. He used to be the biggest slut on Broadway and thought marriage was for suckers. Now he's engaged and looks like he can't wait to sign on the dotted line.

"Thanks, Kingston. That's actually what I wanted to talk to you about. We're not in a rush or anything, but we're thinking about getting married in the spring. And we're hoping you'll perform the ceremony."

"What?" Me, officiate their wedding? "Why?"

"Because you helped us get where we needed to go. I'll always be grateful for that," he says, taking me aback with his serious mien.

"At the time, you were less enthusiastic about my contribution to the situation."

"Your meddling, you mean."

"I hardly meddled," I argue. "I just made you both admit what you already knew—that you two lunkheads were in love with each other."

"Potato, potahtoe," Van drawls. "Point is—it would mean a lot to us if you did it. You mean a lot to us. And we can hardly ask Jack—he'd blubber through the whole thing."

"Well, that's true." I think about it for a second while

the server delivers my red. "I guess so—I mean, what would I have to do?"

"You get one of those internet certifications and write a few words."

"I'm no writer—"

"Don't pull that. It doesn't have to be much. Just write about how much we love each other, how Beck made me fall in love with him by baking me cookies and I wooed him by being grumpy and emotionally unavailable. Stuff like that."

I laugh. "You're the writer. How about I take a stab at it and then you can polish it up and make it sound pretty?"

"So you'll do it?" he asks, tacitly accepting my terms.

"I'll do it." I'm still not sure I'm the right person for the job, but I can see what an honor it is to be asked. I sip my excellent Barolo. "How exciting. A wedding is definitely something to look forward to."

"I'm getting married," Van says, sounding incredulous. "I'm getting *married*."

"It was your idea, from what you and Beck told me," I say, suddenly worried he's getting cold feet.

"Oh, I proposed all right. Beck's the best thing that ever happened to me."

The stab of jealousy is so painful it feels like an actual knife between my ribs. I glance down, but my shirt is pristine. No knife. No blood.

"That's... great, Van."

His faraway expression vanishes at the tone of my voice. "Now, what about you? My actor friend is still single and looking, by the way."

"No," I say, the thought of making the effort to get to know someone new entirely exhausting. "Thanks."

"How's it going with Toby?" he asks without commenting on my refusal.

"What do you mean?"

"He's been staying with you for a while. Everything good?"

"It's really good," I say cautiously. "I think. Except—he needs a place to work. I was thinking about putting up one of those prefab units. I already have the slab ready to go, and we'd only need to install electricity." The idea came to me one day when I parked Daniel in my invisible garage and realized it would make the perfect spot for a studio.

"So he's staying?"

"As far as I know," I say.

"And you two are—" He stops and waves his hands in a vague manner, but I refuse to give him the satisfaction of admitting I know what he's implying.

"What?"

"Friends?"

"Why wouldn't we be?"

"Just—well, no reason. I guess."

"What does that mean?"

"Dude, nothing. If you say you're just friends, that's cool." Van sounds suspiciously unbothered, as if he knows something I don't.

"Of course we are. He's not—" I pause. Finishing that sentence seems dangerous.

Van's blue eyes sharpen on me, his thick black brows creasing together to form a hood of speculation. "You know he's not straight, right?"

"Not straight?" I had suspicions, but Toby has never said anything definitive.

"Bi. He told me a few months ago."

My world narrows to a point. "Oh."

"Not that it matters, because you're just friends."

I reach for my wine and my skin slides impotently against the glass. When did my palms get so sweaty?

"That's right. Just friends."

Van lets it go, but I have trouble following the rest of our conversation. Knowing for sure that Toby's not straight isn't great for my concentration. I've worked so hard to keep things purely friendly between us. I'll just have to keep trying.

NINETEEN

A FEW DAYS LATER, I'm on a video call with a client when my cell flashes with an incoming call. From Toby.

A call. Not a text. It could be something urgent or an emergency. Is Luna okay? Did a pipe burst in the house?

"Deanna, can I put you on hold for one second?" I mute my sound and video and pick up the call before it goes to voicemail.

"Toby?"

"Kingston, hey. I'm coming to Manhattan tomorrow to visit the gallery. Should we get dinner or something after?"

"Tomorrow?"

"Yeah, just finalized the plan. I'm taking the train in. Figured I could take the train back after dinner with you. If you're free."

"Why don't you stay over at my place and drive back with me Friday?" It's not until I issue the invitation that I remember my apartment doesn't have a second bedroom, just an above-average comfortable couch. "Then you won't be in a rush."

"Oh." He sounds surprised. "Yeah, that would be better. I could see the Hockney exhibit at MOMA before coming home. I think I can take a day off work."

"Great. So, I'll see you tomorrow. Dinner."

"I'll leave the restaurant to you," he says. "I know you'll pick something fabulous."

"I generally make everything fabulous," I respond automatically.

"You do," he says, his voice warm and intimate in my ear. "Until then."

"Bye, Toby."

I pull myself together and return to my call with Deanna. "Sorry about that."

"No problem. I think I have figured out the issue with the opening hook." The author on the other end of the video call arches an eyebrow. "You look unusually happy."

"What?" I glance at my video feed, the goofy smile on my face utterly unlike the usual sophisticated curve of my lips.

"Good news?" she asks.

"Ah." Toby coming to the city, dinner plans with him, having him spend the night at my place. It's almost like a date. Only it's not. Only it could be. And apparently my mouth thinks it is, if my hokey smile is any indication. "Promising news."

I HAVE twenty-four hours to plan dinner, and it doesn't seem like enough. I want it to be casual but nice, romantic but not too romantic. Maybe I should stop thinking about it as a date. Maybe I should call him and ask if it is a date. Maybe I should cancel. Maybe I should get a head check.

Problem is, I'd call Pete or Jack or even Van or Beck, but all of those happily paired-off gays are going to either tell me to be careful or go for it. Which are the two poles I'm already wildly swinging between.

Instead, I text my sister, someone who's outside the drama of our somewhat incestuous group. Her dating experience isn't huge—this is someone who's been with her high school boyfriend ever since their eyes locked in third period Calculus. Gary is a good man, and I trust him with my sister, which is saying a lot.

But Luce knows me, and lately I've been having trouble trusting myself to be me.

> Hey Luce, you free to talk?

She calls me while I'm looking at restaurant listings on my laptop.

"What's up?" she asks. "The boys are in the bath, so I have to keep an eye on them or they'll turn the bathroom into a lake."

"How's work?"

"Fine. It's harder than I thought working half-time. Trying not to work too much. But mostly good." Lucetta is a lawyer who took time off when the twins were born and has been working part time since they started school.

"And Gary?"

"He wants to buy a truck," she says flatly.

"Doesn't he have a truck?"

"This one is 'special'—some kind of tow package thing he thinks he needs."

"Well, he probably does," I say, knowing how alluring vehicles can be.

"Don't encourage him, please," she says tartly. "How's your work?"

"Busy, which is good. How's Mom?"

"You know. She seems tired. But she's fine. Didn't you talk to her this weekend?"

I talk to her a couple of times a week at least. "Yeah, but it's not the same as being there."

"So come visit."

"Yeah. Well." The guilt bubbles up fresh in my chest. I can't tell her that I put off the trip I'd been planning because I've been selfishly enjoying spending the time with Toby. "How about Thanksgiving?"

She doesn't reply to that, instead in her most accusing little-sister voice says, "You met someone."

"What makes you say that?"

"You've been MIA and now you're calling me to chat."

"Can't I chat with my baby sister?"

"You can. What do you want to talk about?"

I pause. She's got me. "So, I think I mentioned this guy who's staying in my house in Rosedale? Toby."

"You mentioned him. He's the one who broke up with his girlfriend and needed a place to stay."

"Yeah. So. I think—I mean, I know how I feel about him. I'm into him. A lot. Like, from the moment we met, storybook stupid over him." If anyone should understand being struck by Cupid's arrow at first sight, it's Luce.

"When he had a girlfriend?"

"Yeah. So I told myself to get over it. But I haven't. And he doesn't have a girlfriend anymore. And we're going to dinner tomorrow and I was thinking—maybe it could be a date? But if I ask him and he says no, is it going to be too weird? I don't really want him to stop living with me."

"Is this Toby person even interested in men?"

"Yes. He's bi."

"I guess that makes things a little easier." She's silent for a moment. "So you like him. A lot, whatever that means. You're living with him part-time. You want to date him. But if he doesn't want those things—you'd still want to give him a place to live? Don't you think that's kind of—"

"Pathetic?"

"Unlike you, is what I was going to say. You normally don't have trouble cutting off people who aren't vibing with you anymore."

"It's not that easy. He's a friend. He's friends with my friends. There are stakes here, Luce."

"And you want to know if you can risk telling him how you feel?" She whistles low. "I don't know. Your life has more drama than Mom's stories."

"I've been so drama-free lately," I insist. "I haven't been dating at all."

"Wow, you really like him. Is he hot?"

"He's beautiful."

"Pic?"

I pull up a photo I took of Toby, with his permission, cuddling Luna on the armchair in the living room a few weeks ago, his blond hair messy and rimmed with light coming through the window, his feet bare, the cat in his arms accentuating the lean lines of his muscles. He has a smudge of blue paint on his elbow and a smile on his face. I send it to her so she can see the trouble I'm in.

She whistles again. "Damn. Okay. I'm actually impressed you haven't tried to get with him yet, honestly."

"It's not just about that."

"Oh, Kingston." She sounds almost sorry for me.

I sigh. "I'm deluding myself, aren't I?"

"You're going to have to decide what's more important to you. Keeping him as a friend or being honest about what's in your heart."

It scares me that she thinks I can't have both.

"Thanks, Luce."

"Hey, if it works out, bring him with you to Thanksgiving."

"Yeah, maybe. I'll let you know."

But as I end the call, wake up my computer, and scroll through all the romantic bistros on the Upper West Side, I know that's not going to happen. I'm not going to tell him how I feel. It's too risky.

On the other hand, there is something I can offer him. I'll bring it up at dinner, which we'll have at some safe, well-lit place. And I'll put fresh sheets on my bed for him while I sleep on the couch. He's my friend. I'm not going to mess that up by pretending I can have it all.

TWENTY

MY RESOLVE TO keep things with Toby on firmly friendly footing (say that three times fast) lasts until our second glasses of wine and the delivery of our entrees. I chose an Italian place I've never been to about halfway between the gallery and my apartment. The fact that Italian is Toby's favorite had nothing whatsoever to do with my decision.

He'd arrived full of smiles, wrapped in a baggy rust-colored cardigan and a tartan scarf, a black messenger bag over his shoulder, and it had taken everything in me to hold back from enveloping him in a hug, or kissing his cheek in greeting. If it had been anyone else, any of my other male friends—straight, gay, or other—I'd have given them the full Kingston treatment. But with Toby, I can't let myself get that close.

He didn't seem to notice, and we got seated right away while he told me all about the meeting with the gallery curator. We ordered, we talked, and it was all good.

But now he's holding his fork out to me with a piece of

his brown butter sage ravioli speared on it, expecting me to lean across the table to taste it, and I freeze. Taking it would be like touching my mouth to his mouth, through the law of transference. But not taking it would be weird and douchey. So I lean over, snatch the bite off the fork as quickly as I can, while he smiles at me encouragingly.

"Isn't it marvelous?" he enthuses. "This is honestly the best ravioli I've ever had in my life. I'm so glad you suggested this place. Thank you, Kingston."

I swallow with difficulty, barely tasting the ravioli.

"Of course," I manage to say, instead of, "will you go out with me?" We're already out, anyway. And we live together. What else do I fucking want? Besides, maybe, some actual fucking.

I'd settle for a kiss, actually. Toby's pink lips look perfect for kissing. I wonder if he's a good kisser. Sometimes really attractive people are subpar kissers because they've never had to perfect their technique. On the other hand, he and Ivy were together for so long, it's hard to believe she'd let him get away with being a lousy kisser. She's the kind of person who would give her partner gentle, encouraging, and relentless feedback until they turned into the kind of kisser that fulfilled their potential.

But thinking about kissing Toby is exactly what I told myself I wasn't going to be doing tonight. It's just difficult to keep my mind off it when he's insisting on feeding me, giving me compliments, and fairly glowing with excitement after his big afternoon.

"So, tell me, was Fernanda there?"

"No, but Galia and Grayson were, her assistants. They're very... efficient. And they really do have everything organized. They're lining up interviews with some magazines and maybe the *Times*. They want me to meet with a media trainer, which honestly would make me feel so much better."

"I know a good one, though she works mainly with authors. Do the G-twins have someone to set you up with?"

"If they don't, I'll let you know. Oh, and I have to make a list of people I know to invite to the opening party. Influencers, celebrities, people like that. I'll have to figure out if I know anyone who meets that description. And I need something to wear. I was hoping you could help me with that."

"You mean since I moonlight as your stylist now?" I joke.

"Yes—please, please, tell me you'll help me."

Toby's eyes look like liquid gold tonight, more tempting and teasing than any of the actual bling I have in my jewelry cases at home. How can I deny him anything, even though my heart feels so full of yearning for him that it's starting to hurt.

I smooth down my beard and chuckle, trying to sound casual about it. "Of course. We'll have you turned out for your big night. There's plenty of time for that. Though you could stand to get some outfits now if you're going to be meeting with journalists in person. They might want to take pictures—correction, they *will* want to take pictures." They'll want to show off the artist who's just as beautiful as the works of art he creates.

Toby scrunches up his nose, but it doesn't mar the overall effect. "Shopping is not my thing."

I laugh. "Lucky for you, retail therapy is my favorite type of self-care. Leave it to me." The idea of taking Toby shopping and dressing him like a Ken doll shouldn't be as arousing as it is.

"Thanks."

"There's something else I wanted to talk to you about," I say, shoving aside my perversions and focusing on what I can do for him.

His gaze flicks down to the table. "Oh?" He twirls the stem of his wineglass, then lifts his eyes to me. His lashes look soft. I want to feel them on my skin.

"Your work situation. I know you've started some new pieces, and I was wondering, well, if it wouldn't be a good idea to get you set up in a studio closer to home. Why don't we put up one of those pre-made sheds? I looked into it a little bit." I don't mention I have one ready to order and an installer already lined up. "It's got built-in AC and heat. And it would fit perfectly on that slab. I don't even need a permit—Rosedale passed a backyard zoning amendment a while back."

Toby's lips part and his mouth forms an incredulous "o." "You want to build me a studio?"

"Technically, it comes already built. But essentially. Yeah." For a long second I think he's going to see through the gesture and call me out for being irreparably, inappropriately gone for him.

Or say no.

Or both.

His smile turns bright for a second, then disappears. "Well, I—I want to say yes."

"So say yes," I tell him, because closing deals is my forte.

"I feel like there's something you should know first. Before, well. I mean, I've been trespassing on your generosity for a while at this point. I guess I didn't want to—you're okay with me staying with you for a little longer?"

I knew the offer would force the issue, and I take a deep breath. "I am," I say calmly, though I feel like I've traded pulses with a galloping horse. "It's been... I mean, you're a decent roomie, roomie."

"I'm freeloading," he says unselfconsciously. "But if things go well with the show—"

"Which they will."

He makes a face. "I really want to believe that."

"There's no way the world isn't going to fall in love with your art the second they have a chance to see it." That I know for sure. The certainty in my voice seems to bolster him.

"If things go well with the show, I'll have options."

"You'll be able to do anything you want."

He chuckles. "I was thinking I could at least pay rent."

"You keep me stocked with ice cream and cat hair," I say lightly. "That's good enough for me."

"And now you want to put a studio on your property. I thought you were going to build a garage there. Doesn't Daniel need a home?" He looks at me and I want to hide my face, sure that he'll be able to see every useless feeling in my heart written on it.

"Daniel's not about to make his art world debut," I say. "I just thought you could use the space. It's really not a big deal."

"It's a good idea," he says softly. "I'm touched."

"So we'll do it," I say, before he can think too hard about it.

"Wait—there's still something you should know. Maybe two things—"

I look at him expectantly, trying not to anticipate the worst, like he's getting back together with Ivy or he met Bowen Yang on the way over here and they're running away together. I try not to hope for the best, either. That he has feelings for me, that the way he looks at me like he's always happy to see me isn't purely out of friendship.

"Dessert?" The server interrupts us with the offer of a sugar infusion. I have no appetite, but Toby glances over the menu and orders chocolate mousse.

"Guess I have a sweet tooth tonight."

I wave my hand. "Go for it."

"Also, I'm clearly procrastinating." He shifts in his chair. "So here's the thing—what I've been working on since Fernanda's visit. Portraits. I've been putting together a collection of them for the show. And it all started because this spring, when I took the pictures of your cottage, I took pictures of you, too. Remember?"

"I remember." The day that Toby came into my house and made me feel things I hadn't felt in a long time is seared into my memory. "What does that have to do with anything?"

"I painted you. From the photos. A portrait. And I should have asked you if it was all right, but it was just something I had to do."

I have a hard time processing what he's saying. It's not

what I thought he was going to say. Not what I hoped he was going to say. It's some strange third thing.

"You painted me?"

"Yes. A portrait of you. And I guess I didn't tell you because I wasn't sure how you'd react. It's silly. But if I put it in the show—"

"You're putting a portrait of me in the show?" I'm not sure how I'm supposed to feel about this.

"I was going to check with you first. So yeah." Toby grimaces. "This is me checking with you, I guess. Sorry. I fucked this all up. I should have brought you to see it earlier. Again, I'm not sure why I didn't."

"When can I see it?"

"As soon as we're back home, of course," he says earnestly.

It smarts. Back home. We share a home, but we don't share a life, not the way I want to.

"Okay."

The server delivers Toby's mousse, but he just stares at it, looking miserable. "John Singer Sargent once said, 'every time I paint a portrait I lose a friend.'"

I laugh at that, puncturing some of the tense mood. "Stop being so melodramatic. I'm not mad. I'm... getting used to the idea. Is it a good painting?"

He looks at me square on. "Yes."

"Well, then. I'm sure I'll love it. And even if I don't, you can put it in the show. It's your art. You don't need my approval."

He lifts his spoon and takes a half-hearted swipe of mousse but doesn't put it in his mouth. "I wish I had a picture of it on my phone, but I don't."

"It's all right. I know what I look like." But after I say it and the conversation moves on to lighter things, I wonder if I'll recognize the person in Toby's painting. How does he see me?

Later, I settle the bill over Toby's protests, then we walk back to my apartment. It's gotten cold, and Toby's jacket isn't really adequate, but I refrain from offering him my herringbone overcoat. We'll get there soon enough, and I've already made enough of a fool of myself for one night. But I did get him to agree to the studio—didn't I?

As we pass through the lobby of my building, I greet the night doorman, Franklin, a former college linebacker who doesn't blink an eye at the handsome white boy on my arm. He's seen me bring all types up to my apartment.

When we're in the elevator, I say, "You said you had two things to tell me, but you only mentioned the one."

"Oh." It's dim in there, but I can see a bit of a flush on his cheeks. "Never mind."

I sigh but say nothing. Yeah. That's what I thought.

WINTER

TOBY & KINGSTON

KINGSTON JAMES IS the most terrifyingly competent person I know. A week after our dinner in Manhattan, a tractor trailer arrives on Bramble Street to deliver a simple rectangular building, setting it down on the cement pad that might have been designed for the purpose. A day after that, an electrician installs a new electrical box to power the thing. A plumber arrives the following day to put in an outdoor sink and shower head in the garden next to the new studio, and a carpenter comes to set up a fragrant cedar privacy screen around the shower head. Kingston says it'll be handy to have an outdoor shower in summer, and he's always wanted to put one in, anyway. It will be easier for me to wash out my brushes and clean up outside, at least until it freezes. And eventually it will warm up again.

All of a sudden, it's early November and I have a brand-new studio space twenty feet from my door.

"Kingston built you a studio?" Ivy asks when I explain

why I'm moving my canvases, paints, and tools out of her garage.

"Technically, it came pre-built," I say as I stuff brushes into mason jars and the mason jars into a cardboard box. "He had been planning to put a garage on this concrete pad that previous owners had poured, but he's never gotten around to it, and since I have the show coming up, he thought it would be more convenient. And this way, you have more room for your work!" I add brightly.

Since Ivy's show opened, she's been inundated with orders for more of her dramatic birds in flight. She's even hired an assistant from the Rosedale Art Center to help her.

"I'm happy to have the space," she says. "But—"

I gather up a stack of battered magazines. "But what?"

"Are you two—never mind. I know it's not my place to ask." She sighs, looks down at her fingernails, and picks at the clay caulked into her cuticles. "Forget I said anything."

It takes me a minute to get what she's not saying. "He's just being a good friend." No matter how many times I look at him and wish for more, that isn't what our relationship is about. Every time I think I'm going to work up the courage to say something, to ask if there's even the slightest chance he could want me, I get brought back to earth before I can ruin what we have. We work as what we are—friends, roommates. His unwavering support has me determined to make this show a success. The first thing I'll do when I get my first big gallery check is pay him back rent.

"Toby, babe, I'm not saying there's anything nefarious about what he's doing, but no one builds someone a brand-new studio just because they're *friends*."

"Why else would he do it then?"

She stares at me. "Were you this dense when we were together?"

"Is that a joke?"

"Not very funny, I suppose." She touches my hand with hers. I miss her touch, I realize. Or I miss being touched. "Are you doing all right, really? You don't have to move out of here if you don't want to."

Even if the new space wasn't a lovely, perfectly sized sandbox for me to play in all day, moving seems overdue. "It's for the best. You need your space. I've been trespassing on your kindness for far too long. Years too long."

I wonder, with a stab of discomfort, if I've traded my dependence on her for one on Kingston. But no, this is different. Fernanda makes it different. My work being ready for prime time makes it different. I may still be scared of success, but I'm not letting the fear stop me anymore.

"Maybe it happened this way for a reason," she says eventually. "Maybe neither of us was quite ready before, and these shows are happening when they're supposed to."

There's still seventy-five percent of me that thinks I'm going to be laughed out of the Weiss Gallery when the show opens to critics and collectors, but I appreciate her optimism. "I'm glad you're getting the recognition you deserve."

"Yeah, well." She shrugs. "I'm happy to be busy. But I'm not sure I'm going to stay in Rosedale forever."

"But—the Art Center."

"My board term is only one year. I think I might go

back to London in the summer. I miss it, Toby. And I want to move on." She squints at me as if gauging how I'll react.

As sad as it is to think of her being an ocean away, I understand what she really means. "You want to meet someone," I say bluntly. "You should. I mean, you will in a heartbeat."

"Thanks." She eyes me up and down critically. "You do seem the most Toby you've been in a while. I'm glad."

I laugh and find an empty box for the magazines. "What does that mean?"

"Just that whatever you're doing—keep doing it. I'm happy for you."

"Thanks, Ivy."

After I've packed the last load into the Volvo, I look around the empty studio. It feels like the end of an era. For a year and a half, this place was part of my daily life. Now I have a new start. As I'm leaving, Ivy comes trudging up the path, lugging a scarred wooden pedestal, one she sculpts on.

"Need a hand?"

She shakes her head and plops the square of wood in the middle of the empty room. "No, I'm good."

It's the end of one era and the beginning of another.

I hand her my key, give her a kiss on the cheek, and drive home.

TWENTY-TWO
TOBY

I COME out of my work cave around four o'clock one day in early December to find Kingston in the kitchen making a cup of tea.

"You're here!" I say, my mood suddenly lifting. Today I was struggling with a portrait of Pete, worrying I might have to entirely scrap what I have. I'd forgotten that Kingston was coming up from the city. It must be Friday.

I haven't seen him in a while—he went to Atlanta for the entire week of Thanksgiving to visit his mom and sister and her family, then stayed in the city for the past couple of weeks. I spent the holiday at Jack and Pete's, eating too much food and playing poker with Beck and Van. I texted Kingston a selfie of us at the table with the message, "Wish you were here."

Because as much fun as I had taking part in an American holiday I haven't experienced more than a handful of times in my life, it would have been so much more enjoyable if Kingston had been there. I missed his steadying presence, the weight of his gaze on me across the table.

Jack and Pete and Van and Beck are fun and interesting, but they're also close in a way that somehow makes me feel lonely. They did their best to include me, but they can't help being two cohesive couples while I was their fifth-wheel bohemian friend with nowhere else to go.

"I forgot you were coming back today," I say. "Is there enough water for me?"

Kingston nods and I get out a mug. "I hope I'm not interrupting anything," he says as he opens a tea caddy.

"Just a very poor work session," I say. "In fact, I've been working far too much this week. You can save me by proposing something utterly frivolous to do. Though, I suppose you might have work of your own. Do you?"

Kingston pours the water over our tea bags. "Of course I have work. The life of an agent means I have homework forever. There's always something to read, always someone to get back to."

I pout. "You're very busy and important, I know. I suppose I can get back out there instead of having fun."

"Not so fast. I was thinking we should make a plan to go shopping."

"Shopping?" I lean against the counter and Luna comes up to rub her sinewy body against my legs. When I pat her head but offer nothing further, she abandons me for Kingston, staring up at him meaningfully. She lets out a sharp, plaintive meow.

Kingston, trained as she's got him, goes for the canister of cat treats on the counter and drops three at her feet. Smugly, she eats them, looking over her shoulder at me in triumph. She's got him wrapped around her paw and I applaud her persistence.

"You need clothes for your interviews. Now, Rosedale has some options, one pretty decent menswear shop, in fact. We could start there. Or you could plan to come to the city with me later this month."

"With the holidays coming?"

"It's the perfect time. New York is magical in December." He takes a sip of tea. "Don't you have any holiday shopping to do?"

I had, in fact, been actively putting off thinking about the holidays. In England, I always loved the lights going up around the city, the festive spirit imbued in everything from shop windows to the Trafalgar Square Christmas tree. Ivy liked Christmas, and she'd always make our flat warm and beautiful. The last I heard, she was going to London for two weeks.

But I have no plans besides being here in Rosedale with Luna. My mother's still in Australia, and the last time I spent Christmas with my father I was fifteen.

"What are you doing for the holidays?" I ask Kingston, suddenly worried he'll be out of town again. "Going back to Atlanta?"

"No, I'll send a box of presents for the twins, but I was just there for a good visit. I was thinking I might stick around here. Even if we don't have snow, Rosedale is a pretty cozy place to spend Christmas."

I grin. "Wonderful."

"Jack and Pete usually do Christmas Eve at their place. But my idea of a nice Christmas morning is something quiet and mellow."

"Sounds perfect." I belatedly realize he may not want

company for his mellow Christmas morning. "That is—if you don't mind my being here."

"I don't mind," he says lightly, then pivots. "You're not getting out of clothes shopping. How's Monday? We can drive in. I'll make room in my schedule, and you can take the train back Tuesday."

"My interview with the woman from the local lifestyle magazine is Wednesday here in Rosedale."

"Perfect timing then."

"You have everything figured out, don't you?" I say admiringly.

"Not everything," he says. "For instance, if we're going to spend Christmas here, we ought to have a tree."

"Do you have ornaments?"

"A few."

"We should get a small tree, one of those potted ones for the tabletop. That way Luna will be less likely to attack it and bring the whole thing down."

Kingston looks down at the cat in surprise. "Would she do that?"

"Cats and Christmas trees are mortal enemies, didn't you know that?"

"I had no idea. Well, I think the flower shop sells them. Should we go there tomorrow and pick one out?"

"Let's."

SATURDAY MORNING IS the coldest it's been this winter. I bundle up in my gloves and tartan scarf, tug a knit cap over my head. My winter coat is a white puffball thing that makes me look like a homeless snowman next to Kingston. His idea of winter layers is a faux-camel hair coat, a cashmere scarf the color of milky coffee, and his fine wool sweater and wool trousers, with dark brown boots completing the look. He pulls on a large flap-eared hat that should look silly but just makes him seem like he stepped out of a GQ ad.

"Shall I drive?" I suggest. "That way we won't get any needles or anything in Daniel."

He grins. "That's a great idea. Thanks."

We go to the flower shop first. Shay Brierley, the shop owner, is working today, and his boyfriend Connor is helping him.

"We have tabletop trees over here," Shay says. "And also, if you want something different and out of the box and totally chic," he says, eyeing Kingston's hat, "rosemary trees. They're quite sturdy and they smell amazing."

"Are they okay with cats?" I ask.

"No guarantees that Luna won't want to play with it," Connor says, "but in terms of toxicity, it's fine. You still have to be careful with what ornaments you put on. Nothing too breakable."

I feel better with the veterinarian's blessing, but glance at Kingston. "We'll be careful," I say. "What do you think? The rosemary tree?" I lean close and breathe in the sharp herbal scent.

"It's smaller than I had envisioned, but it is a pretty color," he says. "Is it what you want?"

"I love it. And look, felt ornaments. Maybe we should get some of these. That way, if Luna decides she wants to play, they won't get hurt. Or hurt her."

Kingston looks at the felt cactus, the sunflower in a pot, the tulip, and the felt Christmas tree, then takes one of each. He picks up a big heavy ceramic mug that says "plant dad" and asks Shay, "Does Pete have one of these, do you know?"

"I don't think so," Shay says as he rings up the rosemary tree and the ornaments. "But it's perfect for him."

"You're good at gifts, aren't you," I say to Kingston. "I wish I had that trait."

"What are you talking about? You're an artist. You can make people gifts," Connor says.

"It's not quite that easy, but yes, I suppose I could do that," I say, realizing I need to get Kingston a Christmas present. Something special. Something that shows him how much I appreciate everything he's done for me. Something to let him know how much he means to me. Without revealing how much I wish for more.

But what to get him? I think on it as we put our Christmas tree and ornaments and the mug for Pete in the Volvo, then walk around the corner to Hot Brew.

I can't get Kingston something as prosaic as a mug, and I already gave him a painting. The cottage sits in its place of pride in the living room, and I think it's one of the best examples of my architectural work. He likes clothes, music, books, and cars. But he buys himself everything he needs and wants. Instead, I have to find something for him that he would never even think to get for himself.

I push the challenge to the back of my mind as we order hot drinks from Meadow at Hot Brew. Kingston quizzes her on her and Melissa's Christmas plans. "We'll be at Jack and Pete's Christmas Eve," Meadow says. "You two?"

"We'll be there," Kingston says. "See you then, Miss Meadow."

"So, should we get some lunch? We have leftovers at home," I say, trying to picture the contents of the fridge. "I think."

"We can eat after one more stop," Kingston says, opening the door to the sidewalk.

"What's that?" I ask, noticing he's not wearing gloves. Maybe he needs a new pair. Are gloves a good present?

"We'll go to the menswear shop—just to look around," Kingston says, setting off at a brisk pace. I have no choice but to follow.

"Do we have to?" I'm aware I'm whining, but honestly, clothes shopping is at the bottom of my list of favorite ways to pass the time, just after dental work and sharing an awkward pint with my father.

"Let's take a look. And if we see something promising, we'll go from there."

"I thought we were doing this in the city on Monday." Not that I want to do that, either.

"I try to shop local when I can. It's good for the economy."

"Fine," I say grudgingly. I've never been inside this shop, but it's warm and we're greeted even more warmly by a middle-aged man in a waistcoat and tie. "Kingston, so nice to see you."

"Jerry, hello my friend," Kingston says, launching into his effusive man about town persona. It's quite entertaining, really, to see him schmooze Jerry. I like that side of

Kingston, the person who can sweet talk a lion, but I prefer the softer version of him, the one who reigns at home, unconcerned and unguarded. Now that I know him better, this Kingston persona seems like an act, one designed to only allow people to get to know him a millimeter deep, when the truly interesting stuff is layers beneath the surface. But it's such a charming, beguiling surface, others can be forgiven for only focusing on that.

I feel lucky to be included in the group granted access past the first layer, and I wonder how many more layers there are that I haven't been privy to yet.

Jerry and Kingston examine me critically and start pulling items off the racks—shirts, trousers, sweaters, blazers—and I passively let them poke and prod me, talking about fabrics and colors as if I'm a paper doll they're going to dress up. While they work, I wish with a fierceness that surprises me for a chance to get to know the rest of Kingston's layers. The more I get to know him, the more I simply want to know him forever.

I want all of Kingston with an ache that startles me—an edge that scares me. Because that desire isn't going away. And he's right here—close enough to touch, if I were brave enough to ask his permission.

But I'm definitely not brave enough. What if he says no?

Even worse, what if he says yes?

TWENTY-THREE
TOBY

TWO DAYS BEFORE CHRISTMAS, I still don't have a gift for Kingston.

The cottage is all set up for the holiday. Our rosemary tree is decorated with the felt ornaments and the less breakable ones from Kingston's collection. Luna batted some of them around the first couple of days, then seemed to lose interest, thankfully. We also put up fairy lights in the living room and around the front door. Kingston's sister sent him a huge box of peanut brittle, which we've been doing our best to deplete.

I've sent pictures of the new batch of portraits to Fernanda, to rapturous response. I don't know if that's how she is with all of her clients, so I take the praise with a grain—or a handful—of salt, but it does feel good to know that the gallery show is on track. The opening is just over two months away, and even though I'm not particularly clued into such things, it does feel as if there's a bit of—for lack of a better word—buzz building around the show.

The results of an interview with an old friend from art

school who's now a London-based journalist just came out, and I've had a few mutual art school friends reach out to me after seeing the piece. Ivy was very complimentary, sending me an encouraging text.

I was grateful for the new sweater Kingston picked out for me in town, and the trousers he helped me get at Bloomingdale's the day we went shopping in New York, because they took some photos of me at the interview for the local lifestyle magazine and ran one of me with one of the new pieces visible in the shot. Fernanda was pleased, and I think I looked all right, thanks to Kingston.

The New York shopping trip wasn't even that bad, peppered as it was by conversations with Kingston, who was all excited about his upcoming move to his new offices. His agency officially opens its doors in the New Year and he'll be responsible for the livelihoods of half a dozen people. I'd be cowering in a corner if I had to take on that kind of responsibility. He's remarkable.

And I still don't know what to get him for Christmas.

I consider texting Pete for help, but that seems like cheating. I did get Pete a gift, as well as Jack. I sent a gift basket to Fernanda and flowers to Galia and Grayson. They really have been helpful, guiding me through this process with a steady hand.

But Kingston's the one who matters.

I reflect on the last six months of living together. They've been some of the best of my life—easy in a way I never expected, challenging in others. Sharing space with someone as forceful and particular as Kingston could have been a nightmare, but while he definitely likes things a certain way, I wouldn't call him inflexible. And we've grown used to each other's quirks, worn grooves in each other, I suppose, so that we fit comfortably more often than not.

No, the challenging bits have come when I think about how he looks first thing in the morning, before he's turned himself out to perfection, all soft and mussed, and I wish I could nestle against him to feel his sleep-warm skin. Then there's his sharp wit, keeping me on my toes, the intellectual curiosity that gets me thinking about issues more deeply and in more detail than I usually bother with. I've read more books in the past six months than in the last six years combined—all recommended by Kingston, a little fiction, a little nonfiction, all somehow right up my street. The Helen Frankenthaler biography he brought to me from the city was terrific.

I'm not sure how he does it, suggesting books that fit right into my intersection of interests, but I suppose he does work in publishing. Even though his specialty is books for young people, he reads everything, like a vampire who feeds on words and ideas. But not a scary, evil vampire, one of the sexy, debonair ones. One you wouldn't mind luring you into an infinity of night, so long as you got to taste his particular brand of temptation.

Which brings me to the last challenge Kingston poses.

It's a carnal challenge. I've been forced to acknowledge my attraction to him from the start, but it's become almost unbearable now. I thought that the first blush of attraction would fade over time. But I'm not so un-self-aware that I don't know how much I want him.

I haven't touched another person since Ivy. I've never particularly been someone who needs lots of sex, though in uni and art school I wasn't exactly chaste. With Ivy, things started off strong and tapered off over time. Again, I probably should have seen the end coming before I did. But lately, it's all I can do not to actively jerk off at least once a day—sometimes more. To my shame, always thinking about Kingston, my friend. I think about how he'd feel, what he'd taste like, how he'd touch me. What he might let me do to him.

The possibilities are all so tantalizing, and so out of reach. All I know is I want him so badly I can taste it, and I don't know any more why I shouldn't at least ask him if he could, possibly, maybe, be interested in a skinny American-Brit with paint under his fingernails and turpentine smelling up his clothes.

If he says no, I might be able to gather up the pieces of my heart and look elsewhere for companionship—only I don't want anyone's companionship except his. Kingston's the only companion I want.

Him and Luna.

Who has decided that Kingston is her favorite. The traitor. She goes to him for treats, for rubs, and I think he even lets her curl up in his bed now. She keeps his sheets warm for him and I'm jealous of a cat.

At least there's no human that I need to be jealous of. Despite Pete and Jack mentioning that Kingston has had his share of relationships over the years, he's never mentioned any dates he's gone on in the city. He's never brought a man back to the cottage since I've been here. I'd ask him if he's holding back on my account, but I don't want to give him the impression I'd be okay with him bringing a guy back here for a night or for any reason actually, because I would very definitely not be okay with it. Only I'd have to pretend to be. I suppose I should thank my lucky stars that it hasn't come up.

Christmas Eve, I go to my studio, frantic now over the fact that I don't have anything for Kingston to open on Christmas morning. We're due to Jack and Pete's for their soiree in a couple of hours. Kingston already picked out my outfit—a green velvet jacket and black slacks, a white T-shirt underneath. He's wearing red velvet, matching pants and jacket, with a green shirt. It sounds garish, but he makes it look festive. He's going to make all the other partygoers look like lackluster gifts wrapped in plain paper while he's the exciting present everyone is eager to admire.

Some twisted part of me wants to give him me as a present. I could bare it all, figuratively, at least at first, and tell him that I'm his. If he wants me.

But I don't think I could survive my heart dropping from a great height, ending up splattered on the ground, not broken so much as pureed, if he says he doesn't.

Instead, I take some card stock and my favorite Japanese ink pen and make him a little book. One page reads, "Will de-cat hair your entire wardrobe." Another says, "Olive pizza on me." A third, "Allow you to choose all my outfits for a week." He practically does that anyway, but he'll appreciate that one. A coupon book might seem silly, but it's personal, and it's something he can't buy for himself.

It'll have to do.

TWENTY-FOUR

KINGSTON

CHRISTMAS MORNING USED to be my favorite morning of the year. My mom would make bacon and the creamiest scrambled eggs you've ever had. I know now her secret ingredient is mayonnaise and I shudder to think about the calories in a serving, but when I was a kid, they tasted like magic. My dad would make hot chocolate for Luce and me with Hershey's syrup, dumping what was probably half a bottle in each cup. We'd open presents and I couldn't tell you a single specific item I received, but I remember being delighted with everything, though they were never things like video game consoles or computers. We got practical things, books, a few treats, and it didn't matter because we were together, safe and warm and happy.

Since I moved away, started my adult life, I've had some memorable Christmases. There was the time the guy I was seeing and I went skiing in Colorado and stayed in a villa with a private fireplace and hot tub in the room. The time I flew Mom up to the city and we went to see the

Rockettes and the tree at Rockefeller Center. We ate at the restaurant at the top of 30 Rock and ran into Shemar Moore in the lobby, and he gave Mom his autograph and took a picture with her beaming ear to ear. When Sergio and I were together, we flew to Paris one Christmas and spent the day wandering the city, eating and drinking to our hearts' content.

But this Christmas might be my favorite one yet.

Luna wakes me up, her paws kneading my chest with languid urgency, letting me know she's expecting me to serve her needs in the very near future. Toby's already up, brewing coffee and making toast. I make the eggs, throwing in a squirt of mayonnaise out of nostalgia. We video chat with my sister, crowding together around the phone to watch my nephews tearing into the identical-except-for-the-color handheld game consoles I bought them. My sister passes the phone to Mom. Toby tries to hide, but I drag him back, introduce them. He's not mine, but I've talked about him enough to Mom and Luce that they know who he is.

Family obligations out of the way, breakfast consumed, we turn our attention to the small cache of presents that's accumulated on the table next to our baby tree. A few are from our friends, tokens of appreciation and the season. I make Toby open the gift from me first. I had thought about getting him something extravagant, like an overcoat, but figured he's had enough of my foisting clothes on him. And while I'm not a stranger to buying clothes for my friends, it might seem too intimate. I have to try so hard to ride the line between appropriate and revealing. I think I've done a good job of keeping our Christmas for two on friendly ground.

Instead of clothes or jewelry, I found something else I thought he might like. He opens the box with an expectant smile, which widens when he sees what it is.

"Did you take this picture?" he asks, holding up the photo of Luna I had printed and framed in the city. "It's lovely."

"It's just a picture from my phone, but I thought you'd like to have it."

"Since she's decided you're her favorite, you mean?" he says, but he's teasing. "Thank you, Kingston. I do love it. Now you."

He pushes a red envelope toward me. The outside of the envelope has a big, dramatic K written on it in Toby's decisive hand. I slide open the flap and take out a simple folded piece of card stock. The front has a black ink drawing of a Christmas tree—but not just any generic cut tree. It's our rosemary tree, complete with the sunflower and tulip and cactus felt ornaments. He's managed to completely capture the nuances of this particular tree. I haven't seen many of his drawings, but he's just as talented with a pen as he is with paint. Clever boy.

I open the card and a homemade booklet slides onto my lap. I pick it up, read the first page, and chuckle. It's a coupon for "one freezerful of ice cream." I look at the next one. "Dry cleaning duty—pick up and drop off." There are a dozen slips, and they're all hyper specific, only things that Toby can do for me, right down to "de-cat hair your wardrobe." I look up at him. I hadn't expected anything in particular—perhaps a small painting, if I was going to be greedy. Or a scarf. I'd never turn down Hermès or Chanel.

But this is better. This is something no one else could have given me, and it makes me feel toasty warm from the inside out that Toby would make me something so personal. So intimate, in a way. It leaves me indescribably happy that he knows me so well.

"I love these. Thank you. And I'll look forward to using every single one." It will take ages to use them all up —well after the imaginary deadline in my head of his gallery show in March. Somehow, I have it in the back of my mind that once he becomes a big shot in the art world, he's going to move out, move on. He won't need me anymore and he won't be the first person I see most mornings and he won't be the last person I see most nights.

"I'm glad you like them," he says, ducking his chin. "It took me a while to figure out what to get the man who has everything."

"I don't have everything," I say quickly. *Because I don't have you.*

But I don't say the words, because they'd destroy the carefully curated existence we've built here.

Even so, it's a pretty wonderful Christmas morning.

TWENTY-FIVE
KINGSTON

JANUARY BRINGS the biggest change to my professional life since I became an agent. I officially open the proverbial and literal doors of the Kingston James Literary Agency. I don't quite believe it until I see the notice in Publisher's Marketplace.

Kingston James has left Fenster Agency to open the Kingston James Literary Agency, which will provide its agents with salary and benefits. Stephanie Collier, George Wu, and Julie Davis will also be working under this model, bringing together representation for children's, middle grade, YA, commercial adult fiction, film and television rights, and foreign translations.

Our first all-hands-on-deck meeting goes well, even though I feel like I'm bullshitting my way through most of it. But later that week Julie closes her first television rights deal for the high six-figures and one of my authors wins a Caldecott Medal, which is huge. And it feels like this wild idea just might work.

But one January Friday, I look around the tidy office space I've leased off Columbus Circle and realize I'm the only one there. My assistant is working from home today. In fact, everyone is working from home today. We have a flexible schedule, with the only requirement being in-person meetings once a month. I don't want people to feel obligated to come into the office when they could accomplish their work just as well from home and save themselves the trouble and expense of navigating the city. On the other hand, it's nice to have a place to go and focus on work. I'm glad I decided on the smaller space, though, one that has manageable rent, as long as we hit the projections for our first year's revenue, because right now there's no one at the big conference table or any of the desks. I actually have a lighter day as well. No meetings, just the usual stack of reading.

I leave around noon for Rosedale, looking forward to sleeping in my Rosedale bed tonight, where Luna will probably inveigle her way in. Depending on what Toby's doing, we could order some dinner and I can hear about the preparations for the show.

When I walk into the house, it's grown dark outside, but there are no lights on inside. Luna greets me as I flip on the lamp in the living room, meowing urgently, then padding into the kitchen. I follow, intending to give her some treats, when I see Toby sitting at the kitchen bar in the dark, his head in his hands.

I flip on a light, and he looks up at me, his face drawn. Luna hops up on the counter, nosing Toby's arm, until he lifts his hand and drops it clumsily on her back. There's something wrong.

"What is it?" I ask, my heart pounding. "Bad news?"

"Um, hey," he says. His voice is rusty, and he clears his throat, tries again. "Hey. No, it's nothing. Something stupid."

By his posture and mood, it's clearly something serious. "What is it?" The urge to go to him and put my arm around his shoulders is so strong I have to lock my hands together to stop myself.

"My dad. He heard about my show and wrote me an email. He was—I haven't heard from him in like two years. He was... nice, I guess?" Toby looks lost and I don't know exactly why his dad emailing him would send him down this path, but I hate Nathan Wheaton on principle, anyway. "He implied that he'd like to come to New York to see the show."

"And how do you feel about that?" I ask carefully.

"I don't know." With nothing more forthcoming, I cross the kitchen and fill the kettle.

"Tea?"

Toby nods, and I pull mugs and tea bags down to the counter.

"Let me order something from Nina's. The usual?"

"Not really hungry," Toby says, but I know if I put his favorite order of ravioli in front of him, he'll eat it.

I make a quick phone call to the restaurant while the water's boiling. Then I go to my room and change out of my work clothes into soft sweats and a hoodie. When I come back out, Toby's pouring the water, more color in his cheeks, and I'm so relieved that he's not the zombie he was when I first got home.

"Sorry. I'm being dramatic. It's—whatever."

"It's not whatever. It's your dad. And it sounds like you don't particularly want him to come to the show."

"I just don't know why he'd be doing it. Is it because he wants to see me? My work? Or does he only want to see my art so he can compare himself to me? Does he think it's going to be a success, and he wants to associate himself with that?" Toby folds his arms over his chest, juts his bottom lip out. "Or does he think it's going to be a failure and wants to see it firsthand? Rub my face in it?"

"Why would he do that?"

"My father is the most competitive man on the planet," Toby says bitterly. "It's why I almost didn't even pursue painting. Except that in the end, I couldn't not. You know?"

"I do know." Toby, without his art, is unthinkable, like Luna without her fur.

"He'd want to constantly compare our output, our styles, our successes. I avoided it as best I could. But I never got the impression he wanted to help me get better. He only wanted to make sure I wasn't going to be better than him. So no, I don't really want him to come."

"Can you tell him that?"

Toby makes a face and sips his tea.

"I'm thirty-three. I should be able to tell him."

"It's not always easy to tell people the truth." I think about us, standing in the kitchen, and all the things I haven't told him. All the things I'm too scared to say, all the things I'm too selfish to give up.

Toby meets my gaze through the steam rising off his mug and blinks his amber eyes. "No, it's not," he agrees.

"You don't have to respond," I say. "Email is odd, isn't it?"

"He actually sent it a few days ago, but I didn't check until today."

I lift a corner of my mouth. That sounds like Toby. I check my email six times a day. Zero inbox is the goal, baby.

"Well, then, you can think about it and decide how—or if—you're going to respond. And in the meantime, we can have dinner, and I can tell you all about my week at the Kingston James Literary Agency."

Toby smiles for real at that. "I can't wait to hear all about it."

THE WEEKEND PASSES TOO QUICKLY between tackling the reading on my plate, doing some things around the house, and an informal dinner at Jack and Pete's. Sunday, Toby's puttering in his studio when Van drops by to check in about the wedding. We sit at the kitchen table and snack on a box of Beck's discards. Apparently, he's working on a new blondie recipe and we're the beneficiaries of a trial batch.

"We've set a date," he announces. "As long as you're available—April 4th?"

I instantly recognize the date as the day I first met

Toby last year. An auspicious date, I think. I quickly scan my calendar on my phone and give my approval.

"You better work on getting that certification. I'll text you some links. And the speech, of course."

"Of course. Leave it to me."

"Beck's in charge of the color scheme and all those details," Van says, "so you might want to get with him on clothing choices."

"How big is this thing? I thought you pitched it as an intimate party."

"Yeah, well, um." Van cringes. "Beck realized he's only getting married once, and then he decided he wanted a slightly bigger affair."

"How much bigger?"

"It's in flux," Van says vaguely. "He might even invite his parents."

"His parents, as in the Texas senator and his wife?" I say in disbelief. Beck's parents aren't his favorite people, though they're not completely cut off from each other as far as I know.

"Well, he wants Jack's parents to come, and he thought it would be pretty mean of him to only invite them and not his actual parents."

"Your family will be there," I guess.

"Yep, they're in. They love Beck more than they love me at this point," Van says, but he doesn't sound mad about it.

"Wow, so not only are you getting married, but you're doing it all big and fancy and shit," I say, not above needling my formerly romance-averse friend.

Van doesn't even blink. "Beck's right—we're only going

to do this once. Might as well do it right. It's not going to be as big as Pete and Jack's, but along those lines."

"You mean Jack and Pete's simple backyard wedding that turned into a hundred-person extravaganza?"

"It's going to be fine," Van says, refusing to be baited. "You just have to do your part."

Toby comes through the back door, underdressed in sweats and a long-sleeved tee for the short walk from the studio to the house in the near-freezing temperatures we've been having. "Hey, do you know if we have any—oh, hi, Van." He comes in and shuts the door behind him, but a waft of cold outside air sweeps through the kitchen. "I was looking for a bin liner, one of those big heavy ones?"

I think for a second, translating his request for a trash bag. "If there aren't any under the sink, there might be some in the basement."

Toby crouches low to inspect the contents of the cupboard under the sink. I let my gaze slide over the curve of his ass in those sweats before remembering I have company and redirecting my attention to my phone, where I input the blessed event on my calendar.

"Hey, Toby, are you free April 4th?" Van asks.

"I have absolutely no idea, so probably," he says, rising to his feet holding a heavy-duty black trash bag.

"Save the date, because Beck and I are getting hitched that day."

"And I'm invited?" Toby's smile is wide and genuine. "Cheers."

"Of course you're invited. Beck is beside himself with excitement after you asked him to design a cookie bar for your big gallery opening. He keeps rethinking the menu."

"As long as there are plenty of those heavenly sugar cookies, that's all I care about."

"He's making sugar cookies the centerpiece. Did you know Kingston here is doing the honors at the wedding?"

"I'm aware," Toby says, throwing his smile my way. "He's been angsting about it since you asked him."

"I have not," I protest. "I just want to do a good job."

"And I keep telling him he's going to do a magnificent job. Good choice, Van. He's got the gravity and the élan to make a perfect officiant."

Van looks between us, a curious look on his face. "We didn't only pick him for his public speaking skills, though that will come in handy. He helped me get my head out of my ass where Beck was concerned. Though I still say I would have figured it out, eventually."

"Figured out you were head over heels for the boy?" I snort. "I'd like to think so."

"Shut up. I would have gotten there," Van says.

"Kingston got you two together? That I didn't know," Toby says with interest.

"Kingston is the biggest romantic of us all, even if he pretends otherwise," Van says with irritating certainty.

"Is he?" Toby sounds surprisingly... surprised.

"He's a big ole softie," Van says, and I glare at him.

"Stop ruining my reputation," I snap.

"Oh, that I knew. All you have to do is see him spoil Luna and you can imagine him doing the same to—"

Toby stops talking abruptly, and I look at him curiously.

"To who?" Van asks. My question exactly.

"Er—anyone, really," Toby says weakly. "But, I guess I

was thinking a child? You know you spoil your nephews long distance. What if you had one of your own? They'd have you dancing to their tune."

I have no idea where to start with that statement, but Van responds immediately, hooting with laughter. "Toby's got your number, Kingston. You know you'd be mush around a kid of your own."

"Excuse me? I take exception to that." I feel oddly defensive, not least because having a child of my own one day seems absurd when I can't even get a boyfriend. The one I want, anyway. "It's an uncle's job to spoil his nephews. When Pete and Jack finally get around to acquiring some rug rats, I'll be happy to spoil them as well. And what about you and Beck?" I say, turning the tables with a stab of viciousness. "You planning on having kids anytime soon?"

Van's smile drops but then he shrugs. "Touché. And honestly, probably. Beck's pretty set on it."

"And you spoil him, so there you go."

"You only have one chance at this life, as far as I know. And I don't want to miss out on anything," Van says, sounding more certain now.

"That's brave of you," Toby says, sounding serious. I think I feel his gaze on me, but when I look over at him, he's already turning away.

"What do you need the trash bag for?" I ask.

"Just cleaning up the studio. My manic work period is officially over. I'm taking a painting break. We're working on the final list for the show now."

"Did Beck's portrait make it in?" Van asks.

"So far, yes."

"But it's not for sale," Van says.

"Nope, that one's already spoken for," Toby confirms.

"By you, I assume," I say.

"That's right. It's pretty special," Van says. "Have you seen it?"

"No, not yet." I haven't seen any of Toby's portraits. Including the one of me. I decided I didn't want to see it, though he reminded me I will when I attend the show's opening, a little over a month from now.

"Prepare to be amazed," Van says.

"I'm sure I will be," I murmur. Again, I feel a snag of unease. Toby's world is going to open up after that show begins. He's not going to have any reason to stay here if he doesn't want to. I'm not going to be able to offer him anything he can't get for himself.

Is it too much to hope he'll want to stay, anyway?

"I'll see you around, Van," Toby says. "Kingston, do you still want me to make that soup for dinner later?"

"Yes, please," I say. "And put on a coat, please."

He huffs but grabs a jacket from the hooks by the back door—it might be my jacket, actually—and leaves.

"And you're telling me that you and he aren't sleeping together?" Van's question jolts me out of my warm thoughts of Toby nonchalantly wearing my clothes.

"What? No." I glance sharply at my friend and his erroneous suppositions.

Van just shakes his head. "I wasn't sure I was going to have this opportunity, but I am so glad I get to do this."

"Do what?" I ask suspiciously.

"Help you pull your head out of your ass," he says,

leaning back in his chair and crossing his ankles in satisfaction.

"What are you talking about?"

"You and Toby. You need to kiss the boy already."

"He's not interested," I say dismissively.

"Are you fucking kidding me? He thinks you hung the moon. He clearly wants to have your babies."

"Stop." I stand up and start mindlessly tidying the bar, straightening the books and magazines, tossing one of Luna's cat toys into the living room. I don't want to hear something that can't happen be talked about so casually.

"Kingston, listen to me." The softness in Van's voice is what makes me face him. "If you like him, you should just tell him. There's no reason you shouldn't make a move."

"I—" I don't even know what to say. I can't explain how it's better if I don't tell him so that when he leaves to go on to bigger and better things, it won't hurt as much.

"Look—I fell in love with my roommate, too. I know what I'm talking about." Van could sound smug or supercilious. But he's calm. Compassionate, even, which is infuriating.

"Too?" I echo, my final pathetic attempt to deny what he's saying.

"Yeah," he says, not letting me get away with it. "And while I'm not privy to inside knowledge, given the way he looks at you, talks about you, I would put money on his being just as gone for you."

The flare of hope burns bright and hot in my chest for one wonderful, horrible second before dying out into cold, empty nothingness.

"Thanks for stopping by," I say mechanically. "I have that April date blocked off for your big day."

"Okay," he says slowly. He gets to his feet and drops his hand heavily on my shoulder. He lets me get away with closing the books on the subject this time. "Thanks, man. You be good, you hear?"

"Always," I say.

But later, eating the delicious root vegetable soup Toby's made for me, our hands glancing off each other as we both reach for slices of the dense sourdough bread he picked up from Stacy in town, I can't help but feel that flame of hope flare up again, fanned by the warmth in Toby's eyes, by the cozy domestic scene we can't help but make, and I wonder if maybe Van is right. Maybe there's no reason not to make a move.

Except that I don't really believe him when he says Toby's gone for me. I would know it, wouldn't I? There'd be signs. There'd be evidence.

Going to sleep that night, my belly full of the food Toby made, I wonder if the evidence has been here all along, and I've just been too scared to catalogue it.

Am I going to keep being scared forever?

TOBY'S not around much in February. In the middle of the month, Galia and Grayson show up with a rented truck and a handful of white-gloved movers to wrap and transport all of the artwork to the gallery for staging. He spends a few nights at my place in the city, but he's mostly distracted, working at the gallery, doing press, having lunch with people Fernanda tells him he needs to have lunch with. We barely see each other, and I miss him.

The preview of the gallery show is on a Wednesday, the opening night party the next day, and then the hard work will be over for now. I'm invited to the preview, but most of the Rosedale contingent are coming up for the Thursday party, which will have more buyers and fewer critics.

When I asked Toby what he'd decided to do about his dad's email, he shrugged me off and said he'd taken care of it. I reminded myself it wasn't my place to press him and let it go. But he seems nervous as the day approaches, a little more so every day. I'm busy with work, too, so I can only hope that he's getting enough sleep and eating right. He hired a cat sitter to come by and check on Luna when we're both in the city, and I miss our cozy, relaxed time in Rosedale as the date of the show grows closer.

We have some warm days in early March, presaging the true arrival of spring. Crocuses come up on the walk to work, and the evenings suddenly get longer after the time change. I trade my winter overcoats for spring raincoats just in time for three days in a row of downpours.

And then suddenly the day is here. Toby and I are in my apartment getting ready to go to the preview. I've chosen a simple dark gray suit with a paisley shirt and a shiny tie. I take care trimming my beard, rubbing beard oil through it, enjoying the lemon-honey scent.

"Kingston, a little help?" Toby calls from the living room.

I find him struggling with the jacket we picked out together weeks ago. He's got on his signature sneakers, tight black pants, and a military-style jacket made from a gorgeously decadent embroidered floral pattern, simple black tee underneath. The perfect blend of statement and comfort and very Toby. He's got a similar outfit for tomorrow's party.

"Should I do the buttons up? Does this look ridiculous? Am I trying too hard?"

"Calm down," I say, taking his hands away from the buttons and smoothing the front of his jacket, trying not to accidentally feel him up. "You look great, not trying too hard at all." I smooth some of the curls tumbling over his forehead. "If anything, you look like you're trying the perfect amount."

"It's going to be fine, I know that," he says, his panicked tone belying his words.

"It's going to be so fine," I agree calmly. "Ready to go?"

He takes a deep breath, clenches his hands into fists by his sides. "Ready. Thanks."

"Anytime."

The gallery is twenty blocks away, so we take a car service. I don't want to have to worry about parking Daniel. I splurged on the high-end ride, because Toby deserves to arrive in style, and we sit in the back of the immaculate town car in silence.

"I hope you like the show," he says, almost shyly, when we arrive. The lights inside the gallery are blazing, and from the car I can see some people through the big plate glass windows. I think I spot Fernanda, but then my eyes are drawn to the paintings on the walls. Toby's paintings. I've seen a few of them, but not nearly all, and I can't wait to explore.

"I know I will." If we were together, I'd take his hand in mine before going inside. I'd squeeze it tight and hold on all night if he wanted me to. But we're just friends. Just roommates. I'm not even technically co-parent to his cat; I'm the interloper that spoils her with treats.

We're not together, but that doesn't mean I can't be there for him. So I wait until he gets out of the car and it has pulled away from the curb before I give him a hug—a big, warm, slightly too long hug into which I pour all of my love, trying to give him a dose of positive energy to hold on to as he navigates the rest of this night.

He's stiff in my arms at first, but then he hugs me back, surprisingly hard. I close my eyes to memorize the feel of his body against mine before I pull back. I strangely feel like crying when he lets me go.

"Let's do this," I say, full of false bonhomie.

He nods decisively and leads me inside, where he's immediately surrounded by a crowd, all wanting to shake his hand. Fernanda introduces him to half a dozen people in the space of a minute and he seems to be handling the onslaught okay, responding appropriately and saying something to make everyone laugh. I catch his eye and raise an eyebrow. He nods back and I know he's all right, so I make my way through the gallery alone.

There are three separate rooms, and they seem to be organized by subject. This first room, the largest, has his architectural work, the gorgeous bucolic country homes that by rights should be boring but instead gleam with a luster of realness that makes you feel like you can hear the wind rustling in the trees, the creak of the floorboards, the ring of a doorbell. I recognize some of the locations in Rosedale. He's done one of Van and Beck's dark blue house, front yard overgrown in a riot of blooming plants. There's one of the Art Center at the top of its hill, the white stucco facade of the mid-century buildings reflecting the oranges and golds of a summer sunset.

There are already subtle red stickers on some of the identification cards next to the paintings indicating they've been sold, though there are no prices on the cards themselves. There must be a price list somewhere.

I wander into the next room, which has his British seaside landscapes. These are different, capturing movement in another way. In here, I can almost taste the salt air on my tongue and hear the cries of gulls and the shuffle of waves on the sand. The colors are different—vibrant blues and greens and yellows, a constant swirl of bold colors. I mosey through the offerings, seeing one or two I personally wouldn't mind hanging on the walls of my own home, or at the office. I wonder how much one of these Toby Wheaton originals might set me back.

The third gallery space is the smallest, but it's also the most densely hung. I see the portrait of Beck first, then lose my breath as I realize I recognize every single face staring back at me from the walls. There's Stacy Robinson, my mother's age, the baker of delicious breads. There's Beth, the gray-haired woman who runs the secondhand store on Main Street. Youthful Arianna with her long blonde hair who works at the wine shop. Che, the director of the Rosedale Art Center, with their shaved head and dangly earrings. Familiar, beloved faces, all. But even if I didn't know these folks, I'd want to know them, by the sympathetic, nuanced way Toby has painted them. They're themselves, and they each have a specific quality that shines through. For Beck, it's his amused enthusiasm. Stacy's calm presence is unmistakable. Arianna looks like she's about to tell you the juiciest piece of gossip you'll hear all year.

Toby truly has a gift.

I walk around the central freestanding wall to come face-to-face with—myself. The final portrait I set eyes on is me. Larger than the other pieces, it has a slightly different quality. I recognize my eyes, my hair, the curve of my lips, the slope of my shoulders. He's painted me shamefully unadorned, a simple white shirt covering my collarbone. No beard. I remember Toby saying he worked from photos he took of me the very first time he ever came to the cottage, before I grew my beard in a burst of hope that changing my facial hair would somehow get rid of my crush.

But this painting is no mere reproduction of me from that photo of that day. It's more than that. The person who painted this had to know me. Really know me.

And my heart seems to want to jostle itself out of my chest because if Toby knows me this well, how can he not know how I feel about him?

And if he knows, and hasn't said anything about it, it has to be because he doesn't feel the same way.

Doesn't it?

I don't know how long I stand there, gazing at my own face, but eventually I hear noises—footsteps and conversation as a group makes its way toward me. I quickly tear my eyes away and move to the other side of the wall, not wanting to have to make small talk about this when I feel like my entire world has shifted.

"Kingston, there you are," Toby says lowly, pulling me to the side. He furrows his brow. "You okay?" Then his brow clears, and he says, "You saw it."

"I saw it."

He grimaces. "I wanted to be with you. I'm sorry. This group is very chatty," he says, gesturing to the group of men and women who are spreading out now to examine the portraits. Some of their faces are inscrutable; some of them are smiling.

"It's okay. Maybe it's better that I saw it on my own."

He frowns. "You hate it. You want me to take it down. I knew I should have made you look at it before, but—"

"I don't hate it," I break in. "But Toby. I need to know—"

"What?" His mouth does something funny as our gazes lock. "Oh." He glances at the others, then says, "Maybe we should talk somewhere else."

"All right." I step back. "You go finish your—" I wave my hand. I don't really want things to end like this. I'll put it off as long as possible.

"No, let me tell Fernanda I need a break. They're all going to a late dinner."

"Wait—" But he's already gone, murmuring to Fernanda under his breath. She looks at me and then back at Toby, and then he's walking purposefully toward me. He ushers me through the landscape room, but instead of going out to the front, he tugs me into a hallway. One of the doors there is labeled "office," but he leads me through a second one that has no signage. It's cool and dry in here, a room where canvases of all sizes are carefully stored with meticulous labeling.

"We can talk in here," he says.

Neither of us speaks.

Finally, he breaks the silence. "You have questions, I suppose."

"Just one." My voice doesn't waver, but my entire body feels like it's one big tremble. Am I really doing this? I've been so careful, but I remember what Van said about there being a chance Toby wants me back. If he's right, I have to try. "Do you know how I feel about you?"

"What?" Toby's smile is confused, as if he thinks I'm joking. "What do you mean?"

"Your painting—you know me so well, Toby. We've

been in each other's pockets for months. Your Christmas present—it's—you know me. So you must know how I feel."

"I th-think so," he says hesitantly. "You like my work, you're a supportive friend. You built me a studio. You love my cat." As he enumerates my qualities, his eyes get bigger and bigger until it seems like they're taking up half his face. "About me, specifically, uh—could you tell me, please, in case I've got it wrong?" he asks breathlessly.

"I want you quite desperately, Toby," I say, the words thick on my tongue. Still, they come out surprisingly easy. I've been holding them back for so long it's a relief to release them from their lockbox.

"Oh god," he says as his face drains of color.

My heart's in free fall and I close my eyes against the hard landing that's coming.

"I want you, too."

Instead of a splat, my heart rebounds into my throat. I open my eyes. "What?"

"I want you, Kingston, in every way I can think of," Toby says. There's color in his cheeks now, and his eyes flash with amber fire. "And I didn't say anything before because I thought you were just being a really good friend, and I didn't want to trespass on your friendship any more than I already have done. I thought if you wanted me, you'd tell me. You always take what you want—I thought it would be the same for me."

"Nothing is the same when it comes to you," I say fiercely. "You are not like anyone else, anything else that I've ever wanted."

"But you do? Want me, that is?"

I step close, right up to him. "Toby."

"Yes?"

"Can I kiss you?"

His lashes flutter shut, then fly apart. "Yes, please."

I've got the permission. Enthusiastic permission at that. But as many times as I might have imagined kissing Toby—leaning over the breakfast table, dragging him into my lap while sitting in my green velvet armchair, bringing him a cup of tea in his studio and getting a kiss in return—this scenario matches none of those.

"Kingston?"

"Sorry, I'm a little overwhelmed."

"You, the most together man I know?" Toby teases.

"Not when it comes to you," I admit. "I've been a mess over you since the first time we met."

"Really?" Toby sounds pleased. "As long as all that?"

"I think I've wanted you since the moment I set eyes on you."

"That's so romantic," he says. "I don't know when it happened for me," he answers honestly. "But I do know that I was interested in you before I even moved in. I thought you were fascinating."

"Naturally," I say.

"And beautiful."

"Hmmm."

"And I've wanted to kiss you for what feels like a thousand years, so can you please—"

I cover his mouth with mine, stopping him mid-sentence, so his mouth is already open and the sweet, romantic first kiss I'd imagined is suddenly an open-mouthed kiss of the French variety, our tongues inside

each other's mouths with a speed that has my head spinning and my cock filling and my hands tightening on
Toby's arms where I've clutched him out of sheer need.

It's the most perfect first kiss I've ever had. The most
important one, too. Because now that I know the man
who's become the most important thing in my life wants to
kiss me, too, I don't plan on ever letting him go.

TWENTY-SEVEN
TOBY

WHAT'S POSSIBLY the most important night of my professional life suddenly has the potential to be the most important night of my personal life, too.

Because Kingston is holding me like he needs me to keep him upright. Because Kingston says he wants me. Because Kingston's tongue is touching mine and he smells like honey and he tastes expensive. His flavor is now my favorite thing to keep in my mouth and saliva pools there just imagining getting to taste other parts of him.

Which will be happening very soon, if I have anything to say about it.

I tear away from the kiss reluctantly. "We should—I mean, I want to, but—"

Kingston opens his eyes, but they're heavy-lidded and make me think of sex. "Of course, you've got to finish up, take your accolades, etc., etc."

"It won't take long," I promise.

"But their dinner."

"I'll say I can't come. That way, they can talk about me

behind my back, which they probably want to do, anyway."

Kingston kisses me again, his lips as soft and expert against mine as I imagined. I melt into him, wanting to say to hell with the people on the other side of the door. But I can't. And Kingston and I have time.

I pepper his lips with two—three—more kisses. "Wait for me to finish up? We can go back to your place together."

He adjusts his trousers and I nearly sink to my knees right then and there, thinking about what's underneath them.

"Wait. Yes. I'll wait." His gaze drops to my crotch and then comes back up. "You might want to—"

I glance down and see the result of our mini make-out session distending my black jeans. "Oh. Yes. Well. Thanks." I shift things around as best as I can, while Kingston watches avidly. His gaze on me doesn't exactly make me less excited. "Stop looking at me."

"Why?"

"Because it's not helping," I hiss.

"Really?" He sounds utterly delighted.

"The second we get home you can look all you want," I say, my voice as darkly threatening as I can make it, but he just smiles wickedly, his gaze dropping to my feet, then traveling slowly up my entire body at a leisurely pace.

"I can't wait," he says, his velvety low voice also not helping the stiffy in my trousers.

"Me either," I say with feeling. "Give me five minutes."

"Take your time," he says magnanimously. "Really.

There's no rush. I've waited... I never thought—" He's got that look again, the one I now know means he's overwhelmed. I'm still agog that I'm the one who's able to overwhelm the unflappable Kingston James.

"I know." I didn't expect this to happen tonight. Maybe ever. But it is, and I have to at least attempt to keep my head on straight.

We give each other once-overs and determine we're presentable enough to leave the storage room. Galia sees us emerge into the gallery and pounces on me. "Everyone left for the restaurant. Fernanda says you have to go make nice." She gathers our coats from where we left them in the entryway.

"No, I don't think I can—"

"He'll be there," Kingston says.

"You're coming, too, aren't you?" I ask him.

"No, I'm going home. You need to focus and be the charming artist they want," he says. "I'll wait up for you."

"You think I'll be able to focus knowing that?" I glance at Galia, who pretends to study her phone and lower my voice. "I'm going to be thinking about you every second."

"Good," he murmurs back. "I'll be thinking of you as well. But this is your job."

I want so very much to tell the job to fuck off and take Kingston home to ravish him. But he's right. "Damn it. Fine. I'll see you at the apartment."

"Text me when you're on your way."

"All right."

I hesitate. Am I allowed to kiss him now? Galia makes an impatient noise and I back away without touching him. "See you later."

THREE HOURS LATER, I'm in the elevator riding up to Kingston's apartment. My face hurts from talking and smiling at people for hours, and my head hurts from too little food and too much alcohol. And Kingston didn't reply to the text I sent him twenty minutes ago, telling him I was finally on my way home.

I have a key, so I let myself in. Except for a light left on over the stove, the apartment is dark. I pad through to Kingston's room. The door is partially closed, but I see light coming from within. I tap, unsure of my welcome.

"Come in," Kingston says, sounding sleepy.

"Are you awake?"

The sheets rustle as I walk through the door. The reading lamp on a swinging arm next to his bed is on the dimmest setting, so I can just make him out, shirtless and sitting up in the middle of the bed. "No," he says dryly. "I'm asleep."

I give him an apologetic smile. "That took way too long to get out of, so sorry."

"Did you do your job?"

"Yes, but—"

"Then you don't have anything to be sorry for."

I pause, then decide to take him at his word. "All right."

We just look at each other for a minute. At this time yesterday, I would have bid him good night, then backed out of the room and gone to the couch, wishing for the hundredth time that I could share his bed.

But this is today. And today is the day Kingston told me he wanted me. Today is the day Kingston kissed me.

This might be my new favorite day.

"Can I?" I say finally, walking fully into the room and looking at the bed.

"Please," he says, all formality, but with a rough edge underneath that sends my blood racing.

I peel off my outer layers, kick off my shoes. I pass through to his en suite bathroom, the only one in the apartment. I wash my hands and brush my teeth, take off my trousers, and come to the bed in my black T-shirt and black boxers.

I've slept in this bed before, when Kingston overrode my insistence that I sleep on the couch, and on a few occasions when I had to stay in the city while he was in Rosedale. It's a comfortable bed, furnished in the same hotel-white sheets Kingston uses in Rosedale, sateen finish so soft it feels like silk. I've never been in the bed with Kingston, but there's plenty of room for both of us. In fact, the bed holds us perfectly, as if it was waiting for us to come together all along.

Kingston lifts the sheets and I settle in next to him, close but not touching. It's odd and familiar at the same time, because it's Kingston, someone I've been hovering around for months, someone with whom I feel as safe and secure as a person can feel.

But he's half naked under the sheets and he's looking at me with carefully hungry eyes. He's holding back, still, and it makes me wonder exactly how much he's been holding back all these months that we've spent together, how much was going on under the surface that I didn't see, or didn't let myself see.

"Do you want to go to sleep?" I ask, suddenly uncertain of this new dynamic and my place in it. He said he wants me, but that doesn't have to mean right this very second.

There's a pause. "I bet you're tired," he says. His voice gives nothing away. It's the same tone he uses when he wants me to eat something, or take a break from work, or come on a drive in his absurdly luxurious convertible. It's Kingston's taking-care-of-me voice. I've heard it before. And all the time he was using it, he wanted me, he says.

So he must want me now, too.

"I'm wired, actually," I confess. "But I don't want to keep you up." I stop, realize how that sounds. "Any more than I already have. Don't you have to go to the office tomorrow?"

"I do. A day full of meetings. And you have an enormous party in your honor to go to tomorrow night," he reminds me.

Oh yeah. The opening.

"I forgot," I whisper. "I guess I've been distracted."

"Did something happen at the dinner? Did everything go okay?"

"It was fine. Boring. But fine. What's distracting me is *you.*"

"Oh, right." Kingston sounds surprised.

"So no, I don't particularly want to go to sleep, unless you want to, in which case I will happily snuggle down at your side and do my best impression of Luna. Otherwise, I'd very much like to kiss you again, if I may."

He chuckles and turns to his side. I shift, too, and suddenly we're only a few inches away from each other. His eyes look black in the low light. I think he's looking at my mouth.

"You can kiss me," he says. "I guess I just don't want you to do anything you aren't ready for."

"I've been aching for you for months," I say. "I'm ready for whatever you're ready for."

"I—damn." He chuckles ruefully. "You're calling my bluff, Toby. I guess I thought you'd, I don't know, want to take things slower."

"Slower? When I've been celibate for nearly a year?"

"No one since Ivy?" he asks.

"No one since Ivy," I confirm.

"And when you were together, it was only her?"

"Of course," I say. "I'm highly monogamous."

"Because of your dad?"

"Because I'm much too much of a mess to be able to manage multiple partners at the same time. And because of my dad. And because I think at heart, I still believe in that fairy tale kind of love. If I didn't, I would have thrown myself at you long ago and not cared about the consequences."

"And before her—did you have relationships with men?"

I finally get what this is. The previous partners questionnaire. It's been so long since I've done the new partner thing I forgot there were rules to the game.

"Relationships is a strong word," I say. "But I had enough encounters to confirm for myself that I'm bisexual.

I think after I met Ivy, I considered myself hetero-romantic."

"Ah."

I don't imagine the hurt in his expression.

"And then I met you. And I knew that any label I had for myself was moot. Because I've never felt this way about anyone else. It's the most cliché thing to say, but it's true."

"I happen to like clichés," Kingston says.

"What about you?" I've wondered and now seems as good a time to ask as any. "How long since you've been with someone?"

"Longer than a year," he says. "By complete accident. When my last real relationship ended—"

"With Sergio?"

Kingston nods. He's mentioned his friend a few times, and I always felt vaguely jealous of him. "With Sergio. That ended, and I felt... I don't know. That the idea of trying to meet someone seemed exhausting. I wanted to, at least in theory. But then I met you, and I had even less incentive to find someone else when you were all I wanted. By the way, I've always been regularly screened and there's nothing to worry about on that front."

"I'm glad of that. But you never told me," I say, still confused. "You wanted me all these months, and you never said anything."

"I was scared," he says plainly. "Of losing you alto-gether. And you didn't say anything either."

"I was scared, too," I admit. "Of not being enough for you. And of, well, of it being too good. Because Kingston—" I break off, not ready to put into words how very much he's it for me.

"I know."

I know he does know. We both know what the stakes are. That this could be it for both of us. The pressure is a palpable thing that keeps me from reaching for him yet again.

"What if I mess this up?" I whisper.

"I won't let you," he says. And then his mouth's on mine, his hand cradling my jaw, our bellies pressing together. It's so good, too good, but I have to trust him. I have no reason not to take him at his word. He's never let me down before.

I kiss him back.

TWENTY-EIGHT
KINGSTON

TOBY TASTES MINTY. We have waited so long for this;
I want to rush, but I hold back. I'm the kid with the marsh-
mallow who knows if I wait a little longer, I can get everything I want and more.

So we kiss, slowly. Thoroughly. We kiss like we're
trying to reinvent it, with our lips and teeth and tongues.
With our entire bodies. I've been intimate with many
people in my life. I've had casual sex, intense sex, and
everything in between. I've been with guys who barely
said a word and with ones who wouldn't stop talking. I've
been with men who were ashamed of what we did
together, ones who wanted nothing but my body, ones who
were intimidated by my mind.

I've been wanted, desired many times before.

I've never been with someone I want as much as Toby.

I thought he was perfect the first time I saw him, so
perfect as to be unreal, a caricature of a man, the kind you
might find in a romantic novel, the kind that doesn't exist
in real life.

But then he became a part of my life and I know how very real he is. He's no less perfect for it. Perhaps he's even more perfect.

Having him in my bed at long last, having him look at me with those liquid gold eyes and tell me that the feelings in his heart echo mine—it's almost too much to take in. And yet, he's here under my fingertips, flesh and bone. I stroke his arm from shoulder to wrist, his muscles firm and smooth, and slot my fingers between the gaps of his infinitely clever hands.

Touching him is nothing like I imagined, the times I could bring myself to fantasize about how it would feel. He's not passive, not pushy. He meets me where I am, allowing me close, while his own hands wander over my body, cataloging and inventorying and turning me on with their explorations.

Making out, touching our thighs and feet, our chests, through the few clothes we have on—it's so good that I don't think I could handle it if we were completely naked. Not yet.

Everything with Toby has been a combination of slow and fast. This is no different. My cock is hard, already straining for release, while my head wants to slow down and appreciate every tiny sigh, each patch of skin and brush of hair. My hand grazes over the front of Toby's boxers—accidentally, I swear—and I feel the tip of his engorged cock. It brings me back down to earth in an instant. I yank my hand away and grip the sheets instead of him. God, there's so much I want, and I don't know how to start.

Toby seems unaware of my struggle. "Kingston," he murmurs into my neck. "You smell like honey."

"Honey," I repeat, dredging up the memory of my father calling my mother honey once upon a time, perhaps picked up from one of our southern relatives. I make the connection—I've been wrong all this time; his eyes aren't amber, they're honey. "Like your eyes."

"My eyes? They're brown," he says, sounding distracted. I love being his distraction.

I snort. "Hardly. My eyes are brown," I say. "But yours are golden. Like honey."

"If my eyes are honey, then yours are toast. You know that really dark sourdough after it's been through the toaster oven and slathered with butter?"

I laugh, long and deep. "My eyes are toast and yours are honey?"

"Mmm." He kisses my lips. "Toast and honey are a good combination."

"You are—" I'd say cheesy, too much, and sentimental as hell, but they wouldn't be criticisms. I happen to like all of that. "Never mind. Toast and honey are a good combination."

"Now I'm kind of hungry," Toby says.

I laugh harder, roll onto my back and pull him on top of me. He settles easily but keeps his crotch away from mine, slightly conspicuously. "You want a snack, honey?"

"Honey?" He bites his lip, and I know he's deciding if he likes the endearment or not.

"Yeah," I say, not backing down. "We can get a midnight snack." It's an out of a sort.

He searches my face with his honey eyes, bites his plush pink bottom lip. "No, I don't want a snack. I want—" His hand hovers over the front of my pajama pants. "We don't have to do anything... complicated. But can I touch you?"

I groan at the idea of doing something complicated with Toby. "Yeah, touch me." I've never wanted anything as much in my entire life as I want Toby's hands on me.

He presses down with the palm of his hand, feeling out my cock, which is lying thick against my thigh. He smooths the shape of me through the thin fabric, then looks up. "You're not circumcised?"

"No, never got around to it," I joke, impressed at my ability to form a complete sentence while Toby's touching my dick.

"I'm not, either," he says. "Huh."

He takes his hand away and I ask, "Can I see?"

He hesitates for a bare moment. "I did promise you could look."

Looking at Toby is second only to touching him on my want-to-do list. "Please."

"You, too," he says.

I nod and then we both reach for our waistbands. Toby climbs off me to shove off his boxers, removing his shirt a second later. I've got my pajama pants halfway down my legs, but my coordination takes a hit as I absorb the sight of Toby completely naked for the first time. I've seen him shirtless before, in nothing but a towel. But this is different. His erection proudly stands away from his dark blond bush, nuts hanging behind. The head of his cock is the same pink as his nipples, his lips. His skin is flush with blood and I revel in the knowledge of his vitality.

"Gorgeous."

He smiles, pleased, though his eyes are on my cock, not my face. "You're—Kingston, I'm going to have to draw you. I hope that's okay."

"For public consumption?"

"No, at least, not at first. I'd like to keep you to myself for now."

"In that case, you can do whatever you want."

"Really?" His eyes are on mine now, and they burn with an intensity that makes me feel hot all over.

I finally kick off my pajamas, then hiss when Toby wraps his whole hand around my length and starts rubbing the sensitive skin at the crown. I let out a noise, urge him closer with my hand on his hip. "Come here."

He wedges himself close and I wrap my hand around him. He's hot to my touch, and I smear my thumb around the head, damp with pre-come.

It's hard to concentrate on giving him a decent hand job when he's working me like a pro, even dry. Speaking of —"Toby, honey, wait. Let me get some lube."

"Uh. Yeah. Sure. Wait." He takes his hand off me. "I'm actually, uh, super close."

I lift my eyebrows. Already? On the other hand, it has been an inordinately long time for both of us. If I hadn't masturbated that morning thinking about Toby in the shower, I'd probably be a lot closer myself. "You want me to stop?" I ask.

"No, keep going. Make me come."

It's a simple command, but one I take seriously. I work him with long, firm strokes, then switch to shallow rubs, concentrating around the crown and the nerves there that always make me squirm with the need to shoot. Toby responds as expected, groaning and clutching my shoulder while his cock disappears and reappears in the sheath of my hand.

He cups his own balls, and I make a mental note to play with them next time, because a couple of tugs later, his eyes are screwed shut and he's moaning what sounds like my name. The first spurt coats my hand, but then he opens his eyes and twists his hips and the rest lands on my dick, wet, hot fluid that feels like him marking me. I'd normally take exception to the presumption, but with Toby, I only find it incredibly hot that he wants to get me messy.

He's barely done, come still dribbling out of his slit, when he puts his hands back on me and I realize what he's doing—jacking me off using his come for lube. I almost orgasm right then. I manage to hang on, enjoying the slip-slide of his hand on my length. It's not as slippery as actual lube, and it starts to dry up faster, but it's still fucking sexy. Toby's look of concentration as he jacks me with a single-minded intensity has my orgasm suddenly sparking through me. My balls empty themselves in long pulses that drain me, body and brain both.

I relax into the mattress as Toby wipes his hand on his discarded shirt. He looks at the mixture of fluids on my skin and bites his lip. "You're a mess."

"You came on me," I accuse without heat. "You made me a mess."

"You want a shower? Or a flannel?"

"If you're offering, I'll take a washcloth."

He goes into the bathroom, leaving the door open. He

runs the water for a while. I presume he's cleaning himself up, but when he returns with a wrung out cloth and starts wiping me down with it, I realize he let the water warm up before wetting the cloth.

"Thanks," I say, taking over the cleaning job myself.

He just hums and finds his boxers, slides them on, then offers me my pajama pants. I toss the cloth through the open bathroom door to deal with in the morning, slide my pants on over my freshly clean skin, then snap off the reading light and plunge us into near-total darkness.

Bonelessly, I settle back down into the bed. I have no idea what time it is or how many hours there are before the alarm I set earlier will wake me up, but it doesn't matter. I haven't had an orgasm that good in a long time and I know I'll sleep like the dead for however long I have.

"Kingston?" Toby asks, settling onto the other side of the bed, his hand finding mine under the covers and tangling our fingers together with a surety that makes my heart light.

"Mmm?" My eyes are already closed, but I could wake up if I had to.

"I'm happy you want me."

That's only exactly what I've wanted to hear since we met. "I'm happy too. Go to sleep."

He leaves our fingers touching and then I'm asleep.

I'M DREAMING about toast and tea when the sound of running water breaks into my consciousness and rouses me fully. I open my eyes. Kingston's bedroom is dim, except for the light coming from under the bathroom door. He must be getting ready for work. A bedside clock tells me it's nearly nine in the morning. He let me sleep in.

Last night comes rushing back to me. Kissing Kingston at the gallery, impatiently waiting to be able to get my hands back on him, our first wonderful time having sex, though that encounter feels like the most tantalizing amuse-bouche to the smorgasbord of items I want him to do to me and I want to do to him. We've been so careful to keep our hands to ourselves that there are months' worth of non-touches to catch up on. What we need is a vacation to someplace very boring with a very large bed.

The door opens and Kingston comes out of the bathroom, stops when he sees me. "Didn't mean to wake you up."

"It's all right. I was dreaming about toast." I sniff the air. "Is there toast?" I ask hopefully.

He smiles. "There could be toast. I can put some in for you, but you'll have to top it yourself. I have to go to work."

I frown. "I was just fantasizing that we could take a sex vacation instead."

He laughs. "Maybe someday, honey, but not today."

"So, honey. Is that our thing now?"

"Depends on if you like it or not."

I get out of bed, unselfconscious for once around him in nothing but my boxers. He's fully dressed in his natty suit and tie, but it doesn't stop me from putting my hands on his waist and kissing him on the mouth. Because I can. Because he wants me to. He kisses me back, his minty clean mouth meeting my sleep sour one. He smells like honey again, thanks to that beard oil—the scent of which is going to make me hard every time I smell it for the rest of eternity.

"Say it again," I order.

"Honey," he says throatily. "Honey."

I shiver and whisper, "I like it."

He kisses me, shoving his tongue into my mouth with so much force I almost have to take a step back, but his hand is on my lower back, keeping me steady, keeping me close. But before I can literally melt into a puddle, he wrenches himself away and wipes his mouth with his hand. "Dammit. You are dangerous."

"Distracting?"

"Definitely."

"Delightful." We laugh at our semi-ironic alliteration together. "I suppose you have to go."

"I do," he says, not without his share of regret.

"And I have things to do as well." As if anything I have to do today is half as important as kissing Kingston.

"Then I'll see you tonight? I have a late meeting, so I was going to go straight to the party."

So many hours away. "Not before?"

"You can get into your outfit by yourself, can't you?"

I laugh at that, because he's serious. "I'll manage. You've taught me well. And somehow I'm not nearly as nervous as I was yesterday."

"Orgasms are good for the nerves," he says.

"Then maybe you should give me another one real quick—I think I feel some nerves coming back."

"I wish that I could. I'm already late. But I'll make you a deal. I'll give you all the orgasms you want after the party tonight."

I sigh elaborately. "I suppose I'll live."

"You better." He turns serious. "You have a good day, and I'll see you later. But text me if you need me."

"What if I just want you?"

"Text me then, too."

"Kingston, I—" I stop, suddenly unsure. I want to tell him I love him. But now is not the right time.

"What?"

"I—I kind of wish our first time had been in the cottage." It's something I hadn't realized had been on my mind until I say it, but it's true.

His eyebrows relax. "Oh, honey." He sounds sympathetic and maybe a trace pitying.

"You know I'm going to be ridiculously sentimental about everything, don't you?"

"I'll live," he says, repeating my words back to me.

"You better."

THE DAY PASSES QUICKER than it might have, though Kingston is never far from my thoughts. I do indeed make toast for breakfast, and strong coffee, and eggs. I have texts from Fernanda to respond to. I have texts from friends planning to attend the party who want to check in. I have a text from my mother wishing me good luck. A text comes in from a number I don't recognize.

Settled into my hotel. See you tonight.

Since that could be any number of people, I'm about to respond and ask who the text is from, but get sidetracked by a phone call from Galia going over some details, and another one from Beck asking if it's okay if he substitutes oatmeal chocolate chip for oatmeal raisin at tonight's cookie bar because of some snafu with his bakers, to which I give an enthusiastic thumbs-up. Then there's lunch with a journalist, then back to the apartment to change into my party clothes. I text Kingston before I get in the shower.

Getting ready now. Hope your day has gone well. Mine's been nonstop. See you at the gallery.

I consider sending him a nude selfie, but I suppose doing that within twenty-four hours of getting together might be a bit much. It's just that when it comes to

Kingston, nothing is normal. There's no casual dating phase. No trying each other on for size. We actually live together. Our lives are already intertwined in so many ways. We can't be cavalier because we know each other too well already.

But I think we're on the same page about all that. This isn't a fling or an intrigue. This is for keeps. This is us adding sex and feelings into a relationship that was already intimate in so many ways.

Kingston has become my best friend.

Getting to sleep with him is honestly just a bonus. A very large, very satisfying bonus, but a bonus, nonetheless.

I shower quickly, forcing myself to use the expensive shampoo and conditioner Kingston stocked for me when he learned that, when left to my own devices, I use generic dollar store brands.

My hair air dries while I check my phone. More texts from friends and one from Kingston that I seize on like a piece of gold among the pebbles.

> The best thing I can say about my day is that it's almost over and I'll be seeing you soon. I arranged a car for you, so be in the lobby at 6:30.

The smile on my face must be sickening, but I can't help it. It's still settling in that the boy I've had a crush on forever likes me back.

I send him a heart emoji, then finish getting dressed and head to the lobby at the appointed hour. The Weiss Gallery is lit up like last night, only there are far more people there, plus uniformed waitstaff pouring drinks into chic plastic cups and passing around trays of appetizers.

"There he is!" Fernanda coos at me. She leans in close. "We're doing smashingly well with sales already, darling."

I try to be happy about that, since I know that's the point of this whole endeavor—to make money for her, me, and the gallery, but there's still a sting of sadness at having to let go of any of my paintings.

On the other hand, given the makeup of the people present, it's likely I'll be seeing a good number of the sold pieces on my friends' walls, since they're obviously the ones who purchased some of them.

Friends like Beck and Van, Van looking screen-star handsome in a gray suit with a white dress shirt unbuttoned past his collarbone. Beck's wearing a suit, too, but his is dark blue with an orange shirt—the colors of Beck's Cookie Counter.

"Congratulations," Beck says. "The show looks really incredible. We're so happy for you."

"Thanks," I say, hugging each of them in turn. "It's so kind of you to come all this way."

"Where's Kingston?" Van asks. "I thought he'd be with you."

"Be with me? Why would he be with me?" I say, suddenly feeling like a kid who's been caught with his hand in the cookie jar. Van is one of Kingston's best friends. What if he can see it all over my face that Kingston and I slept together? Does Kingston care if other people know? We've barely had a chance to talk, let alone discuss the terms of our new relationship. My gaze darts to the hallway that leads to the storage closet where our first kiss took place.

My cheeks feel hot, and I look at Van and Beck to find them both studying me with different kinds of smiles on their faces. Van's smiling at me as though he knows something I don't know. Beck's smile looks as if he's figured out a secret. Damn it.

"He's meeting me here," I say, because it's obvious we're not going to be able to keep this to ourselves even if we wanted to.

"Excellent," Van says, while Beck says, "So happy for you."

I can't explain further, because Ivy's throwing her arms around me. "You gorgeous bastard," she says happily. "You did it. You really did it. I am so proud of you, babe."

Beck and Van let us have some privacy, and I smile at my ex. "I was hoping you would be proud, but it's okay if you want to be smug and say I told you so."

"Well, I did. But you know what—I'm honestly so happy that you made this happen. The show looks fab, the buzz is off the charts positive, and you are making a big splash in the best kind of way."

I grimace. "You say I made this happen, but I really didn't. You did. Pete did. Fernanda did. All I had to do was paint the pictures, which I would have done, anyway."

"Stop being self-deprecating and thinking it's only your success if you do everything yourself. You know that's not true. And yes, you painted these pictures, these stunningly beautiful, intensely gorgeous pictures. I quite like the one of me."

"Do you? That's good, because it's yours."

"What? Truly?"

"The gallery knows which ones aren't for sale and that one is not for sale. It's yours, if you want it."

"I want it, babe, I want it. And I'd love to stay and celebrate your success more, but I have a date."

I grin, nothing but happy for her. Well, maybe a single twinge of regret, but the rest of me—happy. "With whom?"

"A friend of a friend. But it'll be our third date," she says, looking radiant.

"Enjoy," I say sincerely.

"Thanks." She scans the growing crowd. "Where is Kingston?"

"He'll be here," I say, letting my joy show on my face on purpose this time.

She doesn't miss it. "Oh, Toby. Again, I'm really happy for you." She kisses my cheek and walks away.

I talk to a few more people, note the new dots on some of the paintings indicating they're sold, take a glass of white from a tray of them in the corner. I'm about to call Kingston to see if he's been held up when there's a hubbub at the entrance. Fernanda crosses the room quickly and I look to see which critic or patron she's greeting so effusively. The new arrivals are a woman I don't recognize and a man I do. The wine glass slips in my hand, but I manage to retain my grip before it can fall to the floor. The man at the entrance of the gallery is Nathan Wheaton, London art scene darling and, incidentally, my father.

THIRTY
KINGSTON

I DON'T HAVE time to go home and change before heading to the gallery, but I always keep some emergency clothes and toiletries at the office. I spruce myself up before I grab a car to the gallery. I didn't have time for dinner, either, but I plan to take Toby and our friends out for a celebratory meal after the festivities conclude.

I'm not hungry anyway, except to see Toby again. The day was interminably long, one meeting after another, when all my brain wanted to do was relive the sensation of Toby jerking me off using his own come as lube last night, or maybe the moment this morning when he kissed me in nothing but his underwear, his tongue making wicked promises in my mouth.

The boy was on my mind plenty before last night. Now it's hard to think of anything but him. His eyes, his hands, his smile, his cock.

The car slides to a stop, double parking in front of the gallery, so I get out quickly, thanking my driver. I straighten the purple paisley tie tucked into my gray waist-coat before strolling in. I spot Jack and Pete first, who are staring at something with concerned looks on their faces, and follow their gazes to see Toby. My entire self relaxes at being near him again until I realize his face has an expression I've never seen before. He appears... helpless.

That's when I notice the man standing near him. He's a shade shorter than Toby, clean-shaven, with thinning gray hair. He's not as beautiful as Toby, but he has an appealing face, lines and all making him look handsomely rakish. He's wearing a citrine-colored blazer and expensive-looking jeans. Loafers. His eyes are the same color as Toby's, if a touch diluted, and I know this must be his father.

There's a woman with them, tall and sharply beautiful, her black dress with its feather motif giving her the appearance of a crow. Her gaze is focused on Toby in a way that instantly activates my possessive instincts. I've never been particularly jealous about my partners before, but Toby is the exception yet again.

Fernanda makes up the fourth vertex of the square, standing out in her ruby red dress and jet-black hair, talking and gesticulating in a way that seems like she's overcompensating for something.

I cross the room, smiling vaguely at the people in my path, and reach the group in time to hear Fernanda say, "Let me show you the other gallery rooms, Miss Field-stone, Mr. Wheaton."

"Nathan, please," he says, giving her a toothy smile. "And I'd love it if Tobes would show us around."

Toby looks at Fernanda, who gives him an encouraging smile. "Fine," Toby says, sounding eerily blank, then his gaze lights on me and his eyes get wide. He holds a hand out and it feels like he's asking for a lifeline, which I'm only too happy to provide. I get to him in two long strides, slide my hand into his, and squeeze gently before letting go.

"Hello, you," I say to him under my breath.

His mouth is pinched, and his eyes are stressed, but his voice comes out steady as he makes introductions.

"Kingston, I want you to meet my dad, Nathan Wheaton. And this is his friend, Sally Fieldstone."

"Fieldstone Gallery, Hempstead Heath," she says quickly in a breathy English accent. "We're *deeply* interested in Toby doing a show for us. I would do absolutely *anything* to get you to commit," she adds, stressing the anything in a way that makes me uncomfortable.

Fernanda interjects herself. "Yes, well, there will be time to discuss future offers later. For now, let's congratulate Toby on his marvelous success."

"Yes, *vast* quantities of congratulations, Toby," Sally says, fluttering her eyelashes. I cringe at her penchant for stressing her words as if speaking in italics. "Can we get a *selfie*?" She whips out her phone, moves closer to Toby, and snaps a pic before he can respond.

Nathan Wheaton offers me a dry, warm hand to shake. "Pleased to meet you," he says, sounding like he means it. "Are you an artist, Kingston?"

"No, I'm a literary agent."

"That's where the money is, isn't it?" he says knowingly in a not-quite-posh London accent. "Not in the writ-ing, that's for damn certain."

"I do the best I can for my clients," I say neutrally. "When did you arrive in New York?"

"Just today, actually. Jet lag is an absolute bitch. I had to practically snort a double espresso to stay up for this, but, well, it's been ages since I've been to Manhattan, so when I heard about Tobes's show, it gave me the perfect excuse. I've got some friends in the city to catch up with. And there are some shows I want to see. Including this one, of course," he says, glancing around. "I understand Tobes has been making every art critic in New York cream their panties. Boy takes after his dad—ha ha." Nathan Wheaton might have come off as caddishly charming twenty-five years ago, but now he just seems boorish.

"I can see why," Sally echoes, leaning into Toby's physical space again. "Who wants to look at the art when you can look at the *artist*?"

Toby looks faintly horrified and Fernanda steps in. "Sally, dear, have you heard about the dustup with Roxanne Robespierre and that collector of Greek antiquities?"

"That was a holy mess, wasn't it?" The two women head for the next gallery with their heads together, and I have to give Fernanda props for distracting Sally with art world gossip.

"The next batch are landscapes," Toby says stiffly, leading the way. I suppose he wants to get this over with. I have no idea what's going on in his mind, but he seems like a shadow of his usual self. He's not the most outgoing person ever, but this is a side I've never seen—quiet and cowed.

"Tobes?" I mutter into Toby's ear in an effort to cheer him up as we walk shoulder to shoulder into the next gallery.

"He's the only one who calls me that," he whispers back. "I didn't know he'd be here. With an acolyte in tow," he adds, meaning Sally Fieldstone.

"These are more like it," Nathan says when we come into the next room with the British seascapes. "The little American houses are quaint, but these are more dramatic. Well done, you," he says to Toby, but it doesn't sound much like a compliment. "Reminds me of my beach series. Sold out opening night, if I recall correctly. I had people begging me to do more. Should have charged twice as much for those."

"Yes, these are very *alive*, very *moving*—in more ways than one," Sally says. She's not wrong, but still, her breathless commentary bothers me.

Toby's only response is to say, "There's one more room."

The five of us pass into the gallery hung with the portrait collection. While Sally and Fernanda engage in animated conversation, I glance at my portrait, still stunned by its power. My gaze drops to the information card on the wall, and I start when I see one of the red dots indicating it's been sold. Was that there yesterday? I didn't notice in the moment. Who on earth would have bought this painting, and why didn't I think to ask Toby to take it off the market? I have to let that go for now, because Toby's dad is looking at the portraits with a curl of distaste on his lips.

"These are... different," he says, looking at the one of Stacy, curvy and serene, her tight black braids so glossy and active they look like they're mid-swing around her shoulders. He stops in front of one of Ivy. She's working in the painting, a smear of clay on her cheek, but no less beautiful for it. I confess I don't love it, despite its obvious aesthetic appeal; I'll never not be slightly envious of the decade she got to spend with Toby before I even knew he existed. That card has a red dot as well.

"Oh, it's our girl, Ivy," Nathan says jovially. "Where's your gorgeous girlfriend tonight, then?"

"Ivy and I broke up months ago, Dad," Toby says. "Though she was here earlier." He glances at me, and I try hard not to betray any envy. "She had to go—had a date."

A date? I like the sound of that.

"You broke up? Are you mad?" Nathan's voice is scornful and disbelieving. "She was the best thing that ever happened to you. Smart, beautiful, rich. You run around on her?"

"No, Dad, I did not run around on her," Toby says tightly. "Our relationship had simply run its course."

"Well, fine, then," Nathan says in an injured tone. "Pardon me for taking an interest in your love life."

My jaw drops at the effrontery of that statement, but Toby doesn't snap back the way I would. I'm having a hard time not wanting to throw Nathan out for ruining what should be a fun celebratory night for his son.

Instead, Toby just says, "So that's it. That's the show."

"Never got into portraits, myself." It's clear Nathan is

the kind of person who constantly needs to steer the conversation back to him.

"They are truly *incredible*," Sally says, waving a slim feathered arm around. "You clearly earned all the accolades that have been trickling across the pond, Tobias." Tobias? My skin crawls at the presumptuous familiarity of Sally Fieldstone, even if I can't fault her for loving Toby's work.

"He's our star," Fernanda says proudly. "This is the beginning of a long, lustrous career."

"Is this *you*?" Sally says, noticing my portrait for the first time.

"It is," I confirm, even though it should be obvious.

She looks back and forth from the picture to my face. "Extraordinary. Absolutely extraordinary. Fernanda, I will pay *double* whatever your best offer for this one is."

"Excuse me?" Why would this random woman want to buy a picture of me?

"It's so *pure*. The love shines through it."

I frown. I happen to agree, and it galls me that the annoying art lady sees it, too. But that's the power of Toby's work.

"I'll pay triple," I say, having no idea what I'm offering. No way is this painting going to her.

Fernanda titters. "Oh, my."

"Bidding war on opening night," Nathan says, grinning slyly at Toby. "Well done, you. Not bad for a couple of days of work, eh?"

"Quadruple. I *have* to have it, *seriously*," Sally says, touching Toby's arm and curling her fingers around his bicep. I have to restrain myself to merely staring daggers at her instead of slapping away her hand.

Toby twitches out of her grasp but says nothing—not about the fight over my portrait, not about his father's insulting insinuations about his work. I telepathically urge him to stand up to his dad, maybe to tell Fernanda the picture isn't for sale at any price.

Instead, he turns and walks out.

IT MAY BE MID-MARCH, but now that it's gone dark, the street outside the gallery seems cold. Perhaps winter isn't over quite yet. I thought tonight would both be a culmination and a kickoff. I couldn't wait to show off my work and also show off Kingston, so proud to be the one he's chosen to be with.

But I just feel sad.

Because my father didn't show up to my opening to be supportive, or to show his love, or to congratulate me on my hard work and wish me success.

He came because he wanted to make sure I wouldn't be a threat to his own sense of superiority and success, or, barring that, to let some of my hot new artist fairy dust rub off on him.

I hate that I was happy to see him, only for a minute, before he opened his mouth and confirmed all of my worst suspicions. And I hate that Kingston will know what kind of man I spring from. The kind of man I could easily turn into if I'm not careful.

"Toby, stop!"

Hearing my name halts me in my tracks and I realize I'm at least a couple of blocks from the gallery, my feet having kept me moving downtown. I turn around and it's Kingston rushing toward me, a groove of concern between his eyebrows.

I move to him, suddenly needing him like a breath of fresh, clean air. We collide softly, his arms steadying me, our jackets padding our landing.

"I'm sorry," I say, putting my face on his shoulder for a mere second before pulling back, conscious of being outside on the street and not sure how public we can be, even in this artsy district of Manhattan.

But Kingston's apparently not bothered, keeping me close. "Honey, no, don't be sorry. Are you all right? You didn't say a word."

Shit. I'm being so unprofessional. "I shouldn't have left. We should go back."

"We will in a minute. Take your time."

We stand there in front of some handbag store that's gone dark for the night. Pedestrians move around us, and I look at him and drink in his face, from the proud forehead to the divot in his lips. He really is regal, befitting his name. He's a prince, a king, the ruler of my heart.

"Are you sure you want to be with me?" It's not what I was planning to say, but it makes sense. "Because what if I can't help but turn into him?"

Kingston puts a hand over his heart, as if I've wounded him with an invisible knife. I feel terrible, making him hurt. He keeps his hand on his chest, but his face softens.

"Do you remember when you told me you were afraid

of being a success, because it might change you the way it changed your dad?"

"Yes."

"Having met your dad," he says with his usual air of authority, "you have nothing to worry about. You may have inherited his artistic side and his eye color, but you're nothing like him. He's vain, superficial, and self-centered."

"I'm self-centered," I counter, because Kingston needs to know the truth. "I'm not perfect, Kingston. If we're together, there are going to be things that aggravate you about me. God knows I drove Ivy up the wall with any number of my bad habits."

"First of all—I'm not Ivy," Kingston says crisply.

"See, there I go talking about my ex. Why would you want to hear about her? I'm terrible at this."

But Kingston doesn't let me keep digging myself deeper. "You aren't perfect, Toby. Neither am I. But you're thoughtful, generous. You make art because you can't not make it, not to assuage some part of your ego. Not for strokes and accolades. You'll get those, too, because you have talent, but I'm not attracted to your talent."

"You aren't?"

"I'm attracted to your work ethic. You work harder than anyone I know—besides me. And I've worked with enough artists to know it's only a fraction about talent and the rest is about getting down to work."

"My dad works hard, too. And plays hard."

"Your dad, no offense, kind of sucks."

I laugh, a sort of watery laugh that makes me realize how close to crying I am. "He does kind of suck. That's why I told him not to come in the first place. I should have known he wouldn't listen. And what about that Sally person?"

"She loves your work," Kingston says, "but if she touches you without permission again, I may have to say something."

"See, this is why I didn't want—" I take a breath, steady myself in the calm gaze of Kingston's toasty brown eyes. "I wanted to avoid all of this nonsense."

"I know, honey." Kingston sounds sympathetic. "But it's temporary. Let Fernanda play interference for you with the Sallys of the world. And if she's not doing a good enough job, you find someone else."

Fernanda's not the problem. My dad isn't even the problem. It hits me then that I am. "She's doing fine. I'm the one who's acting like a child."

"I don't know about that."

"No, that's exactly what I've been doing. The minute he stepped into the gallery, it was like I was twelve again, showing him my drawings of cats and mountains and dragons and wanting him to love them. To love me. But I'm an adult. He can try to lure me into that dynamic, but I don't have to play my role anymore. I'm done with that."

Kingston just beams at me, as if he's proud of me or something.

"I'm not afraid of success anymore," I say slowly. "Because I think I can stay me." I try hard to own the statement and not ask for his agreement.

But he gives it anyway, flooding me with relief. "I think so, too," he says. "And to answer your original question, yes, I'm sure I want to be with you, whether or not you sell another painting ever again."

I was scared of having this with Kingston, in case I messed it up or, in some twisted way, it was too good. But there's no such thing. I'll have ups and downs in my career, and Kingston's going to be there through it all.

The chilly wind kicks up, and I shiver. "Cold?" Kingston asks. He reaches out and briskly rubs up and down my arms.

"I'm so ready for spring."

"It'll be here soon," he promises. We slowly walk back to the gallery, and I'm more than half hoping my dad won't be there, but he is, talking with Sally and Galia near the cookie bar.

Pete and Jack walk up to us, offering tentative smiles. "Everything okay?" Pete asks.

Kingston looks at me to answer, and I let out a breath, grateful for their concern. "It's fine. Just dad stuff."

"I can relate to dad stuff," Beck says, joining us hand in hand with Van. "Do you need anything?"

"No—having you guys here is really nice. Thanks again for the cookies, Beck."

"Do you think I should open a Manhattan outpost of Beck's Cookie Counter?" Beck asks seriously.

"Maybe after the wedding," Van says. "Then you can expand your cookie empire."

"Yes, after the wedding. And maybe after the house renovation is done. I'll need another project then," Beck agrees.

"By the way, what exactly is going on with you two?" Van says, looking between me and Kingston.

"Van," Pete chides. "Ignore him," he tells us.

I smile, remembering that the true miracle of the past twenty-four hours has been finding out that Kingston has feelings for me. I glance at him in question—we haven't talked about this. And these are more his friends than mine, though I suppose they're mine now, too, legitimately, which is perfectly lovely. He quirks a single eyebrow at me —damn, I wish I could do that. I nod back.

"Well, we're..." Kingston trails off and I peer at him, wondering how on earth he's going to finish the sentence. Boyfriends? Partners? Together? In love? I suppose the last one is true, even if neither of us has said the words.

But Kingston, the man who's in command of so many words and can find the perfect phrase for any situation, says nothing. Instead, he kisses me, putting his arms around my waist and drawing me flush to him.

We kiss once, twice, and then turn to gauge the reaction of our nonverbal statement on the crowd. Jack's grinning. Beck claps his hands together in excitement. Pete's eyes are wide, but he's smiling, too.

Van looks proudest of all, his chest puffed out and his blue eyes sparkling. "Atta boys," he says, clapping us both on the shoulder and shaking us apart. "It's about time."

Jack, Pete, and Beck all talk over each other, offering us encouraging words.

I know my cheeks are flaming hot, but it doesn't matter. Kingston and I are... people who kiss in front of our friends. I'll take that relationship definition for the time being.

Of course, the nice moment ends too soon when my father is suddenly at the edge of our group. "I guess I see why you and Ivy broke up," he says snidely. "I didn't think you were gay."

I refrain from rolling my eyes now that I'm trying to be a grown-up around my father. "I'm not gay," I say clearly and calmly. "You know I'm bisexual. Remember me coming out while I was at uni?"

"I thought that was a phase. You and Ivy—"

"Look, Dad, that's enough. You came to New York after I told you I didn't want you at the show. You came anyway, criticized my work, were rude to my boyfriend, and I've had enough."

He flaps his mouth without saying anything, then finds his voice. "You said I could see you if I came to the States. I texted you I'd be here."

"What does it say about our relationship, Dad, that I don't even have your number in my phone? I didn't know that text was from you."

"Can I help it that I had to get a new number?" He sounds irritated now. "Jemima was harassing me day and night and blocking her didn't work."

Jemima? One of his erstwhile conquests, no doubt.

"I don't care about your problems with women, Dad. My entire life, you've always made everything about you. Tonight was supposed to be about me. If you can't understand that, you might as well leave."

He glares at me, resembling nothing so much as a wrinkled toddler upset at not getting his way. Does no one in his life tell him the truth? I feel sad for him for a moment, and I'm sure I'll be working through this interaction in therapy for the foreseeable future. But I'm still relieved when he says nothing else, just turns around and finds Sally. He argues with her for a moment, then storms out without a further word.

I hold my breath until Sally Fieldstone approaches me, an ingratiating smile on her face. "Look, *Toby*, I know your dad is a git, but his name still means something back home. We could do *tremendous* business doing a father-son exhibition sometime next year."

"I don't think that would work for me," I say, not hesitating for a single moment. "And by the way, Kingston's portrait is not for sale."

She wrinkles her pert nose. "Fernanda told me. Oh well. I picked up another one for my personal collection. Congratulations, *truly*." She leans over and kisses me on both cheeks. "Take care."

She's gone in a sweep of feathers, and I sigh and look at my friends, who've all reached some level of achievement in their chosen fields. "Is this what success feels like?"

"Confusion, queasiness, bewilderment? Yeah, pretty much," Pete says.

"Excitement, too, though," Beck adds. "Look at all the red dots on these paintings—there's hardly anything left."

I realize he's right and do the math in my head. Even with the gallery's cut, and Fernanda's commission, I'm looking at more money than I've ever had in my life.

"I'm glad you didn't let her have my portrait. But who did buy it?" Kingston asks.

"What?"

"Who bought the painting of me?" he asks. "I saw the red dot on it."

"Galia put those on the ones that weren't for sale, too,"

I explain. "Like the ones of Ivy and Beck. No, I couldn't part with that one."

"Really?" Kingston smiles, looking relieved. "That's good to hear. Because I can't part with you, either."

SPRING

KINGSTON & TOBY

THIRTY-TWO
KINGSTON

THE BRAMBLE STREET cottage is dark except for the solar lights lining the gravel path to the front door when we arrive.

"What time is it?" Toby asks sleepily, rousing from where he'd been slumped sideways in the passenger seat.

"Two-thirty in the morning," I whisper.

We'd stayed at the gallery reception for a while after the drama with Toby's dad, but eventually Fernanda shooed us away, telling us to unwind, so Pete and Jack and Van and Beck and Toby and I went out for dinner—not at the fancy French place I'd scouted earlier, but at a greasy diner for which we were all delightfully overdressed. Toby had declared a craving for lemon meringue pie and French fries, and I wasn't about to deny him anything at that point. We ate unexpectedly decent food and drank crappy coffee and talked until nearly midnight.

The four of them had booked rooms at a nearby hotel, but after Toby and I said goodbye and headed on foot back to the apartment, Toby looked at me, face shining and beautiful, and said, "Feel free to say no, but I'd really like to sleep at the house tonight. I miss Luna. I've had enough of the city for now."

And I'd wanted to be back in Rosedale so badly it was difficult to stop by the apartment even long enough to grab a few things and retrieve Daniel.

I drove, and he dozed. We've made the same drive together a handful of times since he started coming to the city to promote his show, but this was the first time I could look over at him and know he was mine.

Best drive ever.

I open up the house and Luna comes padding to greet us, immediately meowing to express her displeasure at being left alone for several days, despite the cat sitter looking in on her twice a day when we were gone. Toby drops down to cuddle her, but she wriggles out of his arms and comes to butt her head against my shin.

"She's got her favorite," he grumps, then he slides all the way down to the floor and groans. "I'm just going to sleep here."

I lock the door, put our bags in my room, toss Luna a few treats, wash my hands, and pour two glasses of water to take with us to bed. Then I return to the living room, where Toby hasn't moved, his face still as if he's truly sleeping, a mask of relaxation. I consider nudging him with my foot, telling him to get into bed, like I would have when I was trying so hard to only be his friend. But things are different now. I slide down to my knees next to him, lean over and kiss his mouth, just for being all beautiful and mine.

I lean back on my haunches, watch him flutter his eyes

open like Sleeping Beauty. "I think you should come to bed."

His lips curve up. "You do, do you? But I'm so comfortable here." He closes his eyes again, the brat. "Kiss me again."

What can I do in the face of that request except curve over and brush my lips against his? He immediately starts kissing me back, wrapping his arms around my neck and pulling me down on top of him. I spare one sad thought for my jacket, then decide the dry cleaner can sort out any wrinkles. My hair hangs around us like a thick black curtain as I let him lure me into long, deep kisses that light up my entire body with desire.

His hands find my ass and squeeze, which I take as a green light for reaching down and grasping his cock through his jeans and rubbing mercilessly, the thick denim keeping me from fully feeling him, but I know it pleases him, because he's bucking his hips and panting into my mouth—then he tears away to say, "Stop."

I instantly still my hand. "What?"

"I'm not coming in my jeans."

"Take them off, then," I say, because I'm an intelligent man, but it's the middle of the night and that's the extent of my problem-solving skills at this moment.

He grins. "Good idea. You are so smart."

"I know," I return. "Now, can we please do this in my bed?"

He cocks his head. "Your bed?"

"Uh, or your bed, I guess." I've never slept in the bed in the guest room, but it gets rave reviews from everyone who stays there.

"Is it still my bed? I mean—" He licks his bottom lip, which is fairly distracting, but it filters in that I've said something wrong. He doesn't think I'd want him to move out, does he?

"Of course it's still your bed," I say quickly.

He pushes up on his elbows and I climb off him, sex relegated to the back burner while I redirect blood flow to my brain to figure this out.

"I thought, maybe, you'd want to share a bed?" he says quietly, like he's not sure of my reaction.

I put two and two together at last. "Oh, fuck, yes. I do. I'm just tired. It's been a long day."

"It has been that," he says, looking relieved. "And it's okay if you don't want to share. I mean, we can keep separate rooms, if that's more comfortable for you."

"It's not." I touch his arm. "Do you know how many nights I lay in that bed and wished you were there with me?"

"Probably almost as many as I wished I was in there with you," he says, huffing out a laugh. "We're a pair, aren't we?"

"Yes, we are." I get to my feet as elegantly as I can manage, reach my hand out and help him up.

"All right, then. To bed," he says.

"To our bed," I add.

I switch off the living room light and follow him into my—our—room. He strips down quickly to his boxers. I get as far as my waistcoat when he turns down the covers and gets into my side of the bed. "Wait—you sleep on the right?"

"Yeah—oh, shit. Last night you were kind of in the

middle and I didn't think about it. Are you a right side sleeper?"

"All my life," I say.

"Same."

We stare at each other, at an impasse.

"I can—" He starts to move to the other side of the bed, just as I say, "I suppose I can try—"

We stop. "Maybe we do need to keep separate bedrooms. It's not that odd." I'll do pretty much anything to keep him, period.

He juts his bottom lip out. "And let Luna have you all to herself?"

"I can't believe you are jealous of a cat." Still, I can't deny it makes me warm inside.

"I'm not jealous of—well, fine, maybe a little. But that's not the point. The point is, after months of pining for you, I'm not going to sleep in my bed alone." He stalks around the foot of the bed and determinedly gets in on the other side. He looks at me triumphantly, as if daring me to remove him.

I slip out of my clothes as quickly as possible, keeping on my boxer briefs and allowing myself to simply drape items over the back of my chair instead of hanging everything up in the closet. Oh no. The closet.

"I thought of something more difficult to negotiate than the bed thing," I say, happily settling into the right side of the bed.

"What's that?"

"Closet space," I say gravely. "I suppose you'll want me to clear some room for you in there?" I nod to my beloved walk-in.

He laughs, loud and free, then plants a smacking kiss on my lips. "I wouldn't dream of it, darling. I don't mind keeping my things in the other room."

"Really? You must really—" I snap my lips shut when I realize I was about to say, "love me." "Like me," I finish awkwardly.

But he just smiles. "I really like you," he says. "Now rub me off so we can go to sleep, please."

So I do, and he quickly returns the favor. Then we go to sleep, Luna worming her way in between us at some point in the night, making a cozy family of three.

I HADN'T HAD sex in a long time before Kingston and I first got together, had barely missed it, honestly, subsuming all those physical desires into painting and pining for my roommate-slash-friend-slash-landlord. But waking up a few inches from Kingston, both of us mostly naked, after having come and making him come hours earlier—it's like I'm having a second adolescence, getting hard at a stiff wind and unable to focus on much of anything besides the next time I can have sex with my incredibly gorgeous man.

But when Kingston opens his eyes, he just says, "Good morning," then slides out of bed to shuffle sleepily into the bathroom to clean up. He didn't so much as touch me, and I have a rager of morning wood. Should I wait for him to come back and initiate sex? But Kingston's a little older than me, and a lot more experienced. Maybe he's not as eager for it as I am. Maybe he'll find my enthusiasm annoying.

The water runs in the bathroom, so I get out of bed, go to my bathroom, and run the shower, cleaning myself up but not touching my persistent erection except to wash myself perfunctorily. I might feel like one, but I'm not actually a teenager. I can exhibit some self-control. My hard-on is mostly gone by the time I get dressed in comfortable clothes and head out to the kitchen.

Kingston's there, also dressed in casual clothes, working the kettle and the coffee maker simultaneously. "Hey you," he says warmly, and even if we're not on the same page sex-wise, I'm still so happy that we're together.

"Hey," I say, unapologetically melty. "Sleep well?"

"Yes, actually. How was the wrong side of the bed?"

"I hardly noticed, now that you mention it. Consider me a left side person from now on."

He hums his approval. "Coffee or tea?"

"Coffee, please. How much sleep did we get—six hours?"

"Something like that. I actually thought you'd still be in bed when I finished in the bathroom. I was hoping we'd try to go back to sleep. I already told my assistant I wouldn't be checking in until later."

"Oh! I thought you didn't want—but we can go back to bed now," I say hopefully.

"Yeah?" Kingston looks interested, so I step closer to him.

"I'm actually kind of desperate to spend more time in bed with you, sleeping and... doing other stuff. I just wasn't sure you wanted to."

"I want to," Kingston says firmly. "And I think we need to talk about what we want and don't want instead of making assumptions. Sound good?"

"Sounds very, very good. I want to have a lot of sex

with you as soon as possible, please. Like, whatever you want to do is fine, but I've got a list, if you want to hear more about that."

Kingston's brown eyes turn nearly black as his pupils dilate at my words. "I very much want to hear about that. Maybe we should have coffee later?"

"Later, definitely."

He turns off the machines, and we go back to the bedroom. Luna's not around, so we close the door for some privacy.

We take off our clothes again, while Kingston demands I enumerate the list in my head.

"Well, there's the usual. Blow jobs. Anal—I think I like to switch, even though I've only done it a couple of times, but I liked it. Ivy offered to peg me but—"

"Let's come back to that, shall we?" Kingston interjects. I may be jealous of the cat, but he's definitely jealous of my ex.

"Toys," I continue, "sixty-nining. Oh—and foreskin play. We should do that, since we can."

I stop my little speech and drop my gaze to Kingston's crotch and the distended fabric of his boxer briefs. As I watch, he slides the fabric over his hips, revealing the dark curls he keeps neatly trimmed, but not super short, and his mouthwatering package, not too small, not too big. Just exactly right.

"Not all at once, of course," I say, my own cock filled and getting harder by the second as I shuck my boxers and get back into the still-warm sheets of our bed. "But just so you know what I'm looking forward to."

"Good to know," Kingston rasps, sliding in next to me,

pulling the covers up over our shoulders. "I want to do all of that with you, honey. It's tempting to clear my schedule for the next week and keep you in this bed."

"Tied up?" I ask hopefully.

"For real?" he says skeptically.

"Well, like, for a little bit," I say. "I honestly have never tried it, but I think I'd like it. You'd take care of me," I add. "You always do."

In answer, Kingston kisses me, pressing me down onto the mattress and his silky sheets. His hands are everywhere, his mouth hot and hard on mine, on my jaw, on my neck. "You are a surprise, Toby. I knew you had a lot going on underneath your pretty exterior. I didn't realize it was so dirty." He punctuates the last word by nipping my earlobe and sending a jolt of desire straight to my cock.

"I feel like I can be whoever I want to be with you," I say breathlessly, as he licks the side of my neck. "Is that bad?"

He raises his head and looks at me, face serious. "It's good. It's very, very good."

Kissing him is this blissful act that clears my head, puts me in touch with my body, in the way I want his weight on me, how his legs feel strong and muscular rubbing against mine, the undeniable eroticism of our dicks finding each other, the base pleasure of his skin touching mine. But not just anyone would make me feel like this. It's Kingston, the way he caresses me like I'm something special, the way he knows his way around my body seemingly instinctively. He's never pushy, driving me crazy with light grazes, ghosts of kisses, and I wriggle and squirm, so turned on I splay my legs open unashamedly, begging him to do something, anything, to make me come.

"You want me to make you come, honey?" he says, voice wickedly soft as he echoes my demands. His hand on my chest anchors me to the bed, otherwise I feel like I might float away on desire.

"Anything," I whine. "Please, Kingston, I'm not kidding. I need—"

"I know what you need," he says, voice dark and low, and I shiver as he scoots down the bed, seals his mouth over the head of my cock. I let out a strangled shout, but he keeps me from bucking up with his hands on my hips, holding me down as he laves my erection, inching his way down the shaft. I can see his face, his mouth stretched around me, and I almost lose it at the gorgeously sexy picture that makes.

He cups my sac, tugging it the way I like it. How does he know to do that? Then he wriggles a hand beneath my balls, presses his thumb to my hole, and I'm gone, the merest suggestion of penetration making my eyes roll back in my head, come shooting out of me so hard I feel it in my abs. Maybe I should start working out more.

He stays on me, and I can't tell if he's swallowing or gathering my spend in his mouth. When I'm finally done and push at his shoulder, he releases me, turns, and spits into an empty water glass on his side table.

"Kingston, oh my fucking god." My entire body feels like it's been emptied out, wiped clean, like a fresh spring wind has come through and scoured me thoroughly.

"Is that what you needed?" he asks, somewhat smugly,

as he settles back in the bed. He strokes his hard length almost lazily.

I turn on my side, touch his jaw to get him to look straight at me. "I need *you*," I say solemnly, willing him to understand. We've only been together for a short time, but even before he kissed me in the gallery, I never wanted to be anywhere but by his side. "I love you."

Maybe it's too soon, too spontaneous, too much. And maybe it's not enough because those three words pale in comparison to the emotions bursting in my chest like over-full paint tubes.

He looks at me steadily, his calm friendly eyes reading me carefully. His mouth trembles and he stops touching himself. "How is that possible?"

"What do you mean?"

"I mean, I've been waiting my entire life for someone to need me, to want me, to love me, the way I want to be needed, wanted. Loved." He takes a shaky breath. "And I can't understand how it's possible that it's you. How did I get so lucky?"

My heart feels so good it hurts.

"You think you're lucky to be with me? I'm so lucky I found you, Kingston. You captivated me, and then you became my friend. And I would have been good with only that. I swear I would."

He sniffs—he's not crying, but close. "Me too," he says. "I would have been your friend forever, even if that's all I could be."

"You still can." And then we kiss, both of us moving at the same instant, and it feels like a promise to keep kissing each other for the rest of our lives. When we eventually separate, I tell him, "I'll always be your friend. And I'll always love you."

"You don't know that," he says, sniffing again. "But it sounds convincing."

"I do know it," I argue. "I never thought all that much about the future. I always lost myself in the current painting, the current challenge. But since I met you, all I can think is that my future will be all right if I get to be with you. I don't need anything else."

"I know what you need," he says. "You need coffee, tea, toast. Your work. Luna. Ice cream!"

"Those are nice-to-haves," I correct. "You're my must-have, Kingston."

"Fine, fine," he says, apparently giving in to my stubbornness. "If you insist."

"I do." I kiss him again. "I insist upon loving you, the way you deserve to be loved, which is wholly, thoroughly, and often." I put my hand on his now semi-hard dick and stroke it lightly.

"I think I fell in love with you the first time I saw you," he says, shocking me into stillness. "Don't stop."

"Sorry." I resume stroking, his cock thickening up in my hand. "What do you mean the first time you saw me?"

"I saw you and I knew my life would never be the same. Of course, you were with someone else and so I thought I was doomed to a life of pining for someone I could never have." He rubs his chest over his heart, as if remembering how much that hurt. I straddle him, nestling my soft cock against his hard one, then press a kiss to his heart and put my ear to his chest, listening to the reassuringly regular thump.

"You have me now," I say to his chest.

"I'm still getting used to it."

I lift my head and look at the man I love, who loves me back. That's what he said, isn't it? That he fell in love with me the first time he saw me? "So, you love me, then?"

He crushes me to him, wrapping his strong arms around my body and holding me tight. "I love you," he whispers fiercely into my ear. "I love you, Toby. And I don't need anything else, either."

I hug him back, tight, because he's right—how lucky are we that we found each other—friends, lovers, and both in this up to our eyeballs.

"What about books? Champagne? Luna?" I tease, rocking my hips until I can feel his stiff length along my perineum and crack.

"All nice-to-haves," he says, "like blow jobs and coffee. I can live without them."

"But it's good that you don't have to," I say. "Not as long as I'm around."

He lifts an eyebrow at me. "Oh, yeah?"

"Because I'm going to give you a blow job and then make you coffee. Not vouching for the quality of either—I haven't blown anyone since, like, six Taylor Swift albums ago, not counting the re-recordings."

He laughs. "You make great coffee. And honestly, with a mouth like yours, I don't think you're capable of a bad blow job."

I lick my lips deliberately, purse them, then ask faux innocently, "What do you mean, a mouth like mine?"

Kingston takes my bait and calls my bluff. His eyes gleam, and he taps my bottom lip with the tip of his index finger. "I mean the kind of mouth that makes me hard just by looking at it. The kind of mouth that should have my cock in it as often as possible. The kind of mouth that can make anyone do anything. Your mouth is a superpower, Toby." He kisses me briefly, hard. "Now use it to blow me."

I chuckle and lower myself down, settling happily over his cock. I really don't have a lot of experience with this, but I've seen plenty of porn, if that counts for anything. I start by playing with the head, licking the foreskin, reveling in the musky salty-sweet flavor, loving Kingston's taste, his smell. It's masculine and good and makes my mouth water and my cock pay attention.

I take more of him in my mouth, the velvety weight sliding pleasantly against my tongue, then glance up and am gratified to see Kingston's eyes trained on me like he can't look away. I want to do right by him, and I sink down his shaft as far as I can before my gag reflex is activated by his glans hitting my gullet.

"Easy, easy," he croons as I pull off and cough. "Don't hurt yourself, honey."

I glare at him. "I'm fine."

"You are that," he says, looking over my shoulder, gaze settling on my naked ass. I twitch it back and forth and he grins. "But don't overdo it."

I don't respond, just go back to work, fitting him in my mouth, getting comfortable with the weight and stretch. I hollow out my cheeks and actually suck, and he makes a noise, so I do it again. Then I remember I have hands I can get in on the action. I wrap one around the base of his shaft, the other I use to play with his balls a little, the way I like it. In response, he starts slowly thrusting, keeping his movements shallow, while I alternate licking and sucking.

"That's it," he says, his hands moving to my hair. The sensation of his hands on my head, his cock filling up my mouth, is so fucking erotic I'd be happy to stay this way forever, safe and surrounded by Kingston.

Some amount of blissful time passes this way. When I start feeling the ache in my jaw, I glance up again. Kingston's looking down at me with so much tenderness it makes me crave his mouth on mine, but I have a job to finish.

I take more of him, until I think I might choke, then open my mouth wider and start jacking him into the back of my throat. The wet squelch of my hand on his cock and the head of it landing repeatedly in the wet cavern of my hot, open mouth has my cock pulse with the need to be touched but I leave it alone as Kingston mutters a string of curse words followed by, "Hot, so hot. Your mouth, hottest thing I've ever seen. You want me to come in your hot little mouth?"

I moan enthusiastically in response, and Kingston tightens his hand in my hair. The other's squeezing my shoulder like he's trying to leave a bruise, and I want that more than anything. I want him to mark me, because he can, because we're in this together and he's entitled to whatever he wants. It's so fucking hot the way he's gripping me and the way my jaw aches and how badly I want to taste him.

My own recently spent cock is straining against the sheets, which I'm practically humping as I keep jacking his cock. The first splash of seed on my tongue is so shocking I almost lose my rhythm, but I hold it together as Kingston unloads, coating the back of my throat. He's panting and groaning, his eyes shut tight, and I take my hand off his cock, let it slide out of my mouth wetly, then I swallow everything he's given me because I don't have time for anything else. I flop over on my back, still swallowing, and touch myself, pumping my own length dry, feeling the echo of Kingston's grip on my shoulder, in my hair. I need that grounding to get there.

I lick my lips, salty and hot, and beg, "Touch me, anywhere, please." And then his big, strong, gentle hands are on my torso. "Harder."

He pushes me into the bed, holding me down while I strip my cock in a blur, the orgasm bursting through me, out of me, all my cells singing in pleasure radiating from where Kingston's hands are pressing me relentlessly into the bed. I vaguely register wetness on my belly, breathing too hard to care. Then Kingston's above me, pressing me into the mattress not just with his hands but with his entire body, his lips on mine, kissing with the same desperation I've felt since the very first time.

"Toby," he says between kisses. "Toby, how did you do that? You're unbelievable."

"Sorry, I just got really turned on," I say, catching my breath.

"What the fuck are you apologizing for, honey?" He kisses me again. "What did I tell you? This mouth is your superpower."

"Glad you liked it," I say. "I saw it in a porno once and always wanted to try it."

His chuckle is warm and deep. "You can try anything you want on me."

"I'll keep that in mind." We lie there, halfway down the bed, naked and sticky, and I'm so happy I feel like I could cry. But I don't, because there's a scratching at the door, and a mournful meow from the other side.

"Your cat wants attention," Kingston says, splaying his hand on my chest, making me feel owned in the best way possible.

"Our cat," I correct. "She's half yours now, mate."

"Really?" It's cute how excited he sounds about it.

"She and I are a package deal."

"Excellent," Kingston says. "Now, about that coffee you mentioned?"

IT'S SPRING AT LAST—AGAIN.

The cherry blossoms are in full bloom and this morning it's even warm enough to eat breakfast on the patio. Toby and I pull the heavy outdoor chairs close together, his feet in my lap as I read through a manuscript and sip my coffee, while he pages through a thick art supplies catalog, circling various paints and brushes with a permanent marker. It's a lot like a dozen other breakfasts we've shared over the past year, only this time I'm allowed to absently stroke the thin skin over his ankle as I read and he can playfully rub my soft dick through my sweatpants with the sole of his foot when he gets bored.

"You planning on giving me an actual foot job?" I ask finally, when I've chubbed up substantially and had to reread a paragraph three times before giving up.

"Huh? Oh, not really," Toby says, looking mischievous and guilty at the same time. "I was actually thinking about—"

"What?" I've come to learn that Toby has wonderful—

if sometimes surprising—ideas about what to try in bed. He wants to give everything a fair shot. I thought I was over experimentation, but it's different when it's with him. Everything's new. Everything's better.

"I really want to draw you," he says, like a confession.

"Anytime." I don't mind being Toby's model or his inspiration. It satisfies some primal instinct that wants his attention on me—and only on me—always.

"Naked, though?" he says carefully. "On your green velvet chair. Erect."

That gives me pause. "You want to draw me... hard?"

"Just for me. Not to share. Unless you'd be okay with that."

"One thing at a time, honey."

"I'm kind of obsessed with your body. And your cock. And you, obviously," he says. "And it's something I need to get out of my system."

"You're saying you need to draw me naked and hard for your creative process?"

"Exactly. I need to do this to free up my creative process," he agrees, nodding vigorously. "It's all about the art, I swear." He bites his lip and looks at me hopefully.

I crack after five seconds. "You just want to draw your own personal pornography. Pervert," I add affectionately.

"I didn't say I'd take pictures. Or video. Though I could. It could be a multimedia record of the gloriousness that is Kingston James."

"I'm beginning to get the feeling that you only love me for my body."

"Not true," Toby says, wriggling out of his chair and dropping onto my lap. He kisses me square on the mouth.

I'll never not be amazed that this beautiful creature wants to kiss me. "I love you for your mind an equal amount."

"Uh-huh. Very convincing."

"I do," he protests. "You're the whole package, Kingston James." He squeezes me through my sweats. "I just happen to be hung up on your actual package at the moment."

I'm not exactly mad about it. "I'd be honored if you drew me. Not sure about the erect part. You might have to help me out in that department. Fluff me up."

"I will be the best fluffer ever," he promises. He kisses me again and hops off my lap. "Thank you. This is going to be amazing."

"Wait—where are you going?"

"To get dressed. Don't we have to leave for the wedding soon?"

Shit. The wedding. I jump to my feet, jostling my coffee and spilling it on the table. I ignore the mess and pick up my phone to check the time. "Holy shit. We have to get dressed right now." Beck and Van are getting married today. And I'm marrying them.

Toby grins. "Better get a move on."

THE SKY IS AN ALMOST corny robin's egg blue dotted by cartoonishly perfect scudding fluffy clouds. A breeze stirs the bright new green leaves of the trees in Jack and Pete's backyard. It's the perfect day for a wedding.

I look over the assembled group and smile, forgetting to be nervous when I see everyone's shining, happy faces gazing back at me. There are Meadow and Melissa, contrasting in black and white outfits. Beck's parents are here—the senator and his wife, who are rather stiff-backed, but smiling—sitting next to Jack's parents, who I've met several times before and who appear animated and excited. Van's parents and sister and her crew are there, the little ones squirming but behaving. Beck's employees at the Cookie Counter sit behind friends from the Art Center. And the Rosedale contingent is out in full force— all the nice, handsome gays Jack's managed to talk into staying and making Rosedale even more fabulous than it already was—Charlie and Drew, Shay and Connor. And of course, Jack and Pete, standing up proudly, Pete on Van's side, and Jack on Beck's. Beck and Van are both wearing summer-weight suits. Beck's is dark blue, with a light blue tie; Van's is light blue with a dark blue tie. They complement each other in every way, including Beck's light hair to Van's dark. I've chosen my suit carefully, light gray with purple accents. It's a small wedding party, but a meaningful one. I've never officiated a wedding before, but nearly everyone I see is a friend, so I don't take long to find my voice.

Besides, the only person I care about impressing is beaming at me from the front row. Toby's wearing the outfit I helped him pick out—gray trousers, purple trainers, as he insists on calling his sneakers, and a purple blazer over a gray T-shirt. He looks arty and hot, and the way he's smiling at me now has my heart going all pitter-patter when I should be focusing on my task. Our interrupted morning foreplay has me aching to get him somewhere private, but that'll keep for now. I give him a brief wink, look at my notes. The music—a selection from Vivaldi's "Spring"—comes to a close, and I begin.

"When Donovan and Beck told me they were getting married, they also told me they wanted to do it here." I gesture to the backyard. "This is the place where they fell in love. Two summers ago, they were both here ostensibly to take care of Cleo." Jack and Pete's dog barks when she hears her name and the crowd laughs. "But they were really, each in a different way, hiding out from the world for a while." Beck and Donovan smile shyly at each other, and I can already see tears gathering in Beck's eyes. Dammit. I need to get through this without crying myself.

I take a deep breath and keep going. "While they were hiding, they found something else—someone else. Someone who they didn't have to hide around, someone they could be themselves with. Someone to laugh with, and cry with, and play poker with." More laughter. Okay, maybe I can do this.

"It isn't always easy to admit when you've found something special. The stakes suddenly become high, they become real. It can be scary to fall in love." I glance at Toby, whose face is alight with so much love I nearly choke up, but somehow I manage to keep going without losing my shit. "I'm proud to say I played a small role in preventing these two from giving in to the fear and encouraging them to go after the good stuff—because what I do know, from personal experience, is it's worth it to not let the fear of losing something good keep you from having something great."

For a second, my soul freezes at the thought of what today would be like if I hadn't told Toby how I feel about him—if we were attending this wedding as friends instead of lovers. It would have been okay. Good, even. But this is better. This is truly amazing.

"Anyone who knows them knows that Beck and Donovan have something great. Over the past two years, they've built a business, restored a home, found their own dog to take care of— yes, I'm talking about you, Molly." Their rescue pup wags her tail where she's chilling in the grass next to Jack. "They've built a life together, a life they'll walk through together as husbands from this day on. I'm grateful to know them, I'm honored to be a part of this beautiful ceremony on this glorious day, and I know everyone here loves you two as much as I do, which means you've got an ocean of love behind you to set you on this path to the future. Beck and Donovan, are you ready to get married?"

Beck blows his nose on a vintage white cotton handkerchief and nods. Van, a bit red-eyed, but with a clear voice booms, "Hell yes!"

The rest of the ceremony is filled with more laughter and tears and romantic words from two people who are very much in love. I have no idea if Toby and I will be standing where Beck and Donovan are one day, but I know that right now, today, I'm the happiest man in Rosedale. Well, if we don't count the actual grooms.

When I pronounce them husbands and invite them to kiss, the entire audience whoops and hollers, and a storm of white rose petals rains down on the kissing couple from the folks sitting in the front row. Shay clearly armed them in advance.

As music plays, a photographer whisks Beck and

Donovan away for couple's pictures while a uniformed server appears with glasses of bubbly. Toby bounds over to me with a glass in hand and wraps his arms around me. "You were incredible. There wasn't a dry eye in the yard!"

I laugh and keep my arm around his waist while taking a grateful sip of champagne. Now that the deed is done, I feel a little shaky. "Really? Did I do right by them?"

"You killed it," Pete says, hugging me around the neck. "And now you get to relax."

"Whew." I wipe imaginary sweat from my brow, only to find actual sweat there. "Damn. That was stressful."

"You did amazing," Jack echoes, handing me a napkin, which I use to dab my head. "I mean, our wedding was pretty awesome, but this one was exactly the same amount of awesome."

"Not that it's a competition, right, babe?" Pete says pointedly.

"No, of course not. This is totally different. This is a spring wedding, for one thing," Jack says hastily.

"So, I heard from Fernanda that your show completely sold out," Pete says to my boyfriend. "Congrats. What's next for Toby Wheaton, hot new artist?"

Toby grimaces. "Yeah, thanks. It's all a bit overwhelming, actually. I think I'm going to take a break." He glances at me. "Refill the well, that sort of thing. I didn't put up absolutely everything in my collection, so Fernanda's going to swap some of the sold pieces out at the gallery."

"Give the people what they want," Pete says. "Ride this high as long as you can."

"Good advice, thanks, man. Oh, I'm going to grab us

some of those bacon date things." Toby lopes across the yard to intercept a server with a tray of canapés.

"And how's the Kingston James Literary Agency doing?" Jack asks.

"It's humming along. Reed's YA book went back for a second printing, so that's good."

"I devoured that book. When's the next one coming out?"

"Patience," I say. "It'll be ready when it's ready."

"Agent speak for he hasn't finished it yet," Jack says.

"What about you two? I'm waiting for the next book in your contract," I say mildly. I'm not worried about getting it, but I'm not going to pass up a chance to remind them.

"About that—" Pete starts.

"We wanted to talk to you—"

I wasn't worried before, but now I'm starting to sweat again.

"Should we really be talking work at a wedding?" Pete says to his husband.

"This will be quick. We'll have this book done by summer, like I told you," Jack says, and I internally breathe a sigh of relief. "But we want to hold off on extending the contract."

"Why?"

Pete and Jack exchange a glance. "We're starting the adoption process, and we want to keep our timing flexible."

"Oh my goodness." I grin and gather them both into a hug. "That's so exciting. I'm so happy for you. Does this mean I'm going to be an uncle?"

"You already are an uncle," Jack points out. "But yes. If everything works out."

"Which it will. You guys are going to be amazing dads."

Jack's cheeks are stretched painfully wide with his smile. "We're actually incredibly excited, even though it's all paperwork and background checks and lawyers at this point."

"You should be." I raise my glass. "To this next, very exciting chapter."

Pete and Jack clink their glasses to mine. Toby walks up carrying four bacon wrapped dates and offers them to us. I take one, feeling famished with the stress of performing the wedding finally behind me. The snack is chewy-salty-sweet and I watch Toby's mouth as he eats his, wanting him with a fierceness that makes my skin feel tight. I'm so lucky I found him. What would I ever do if I lost him?

He catches my gaze with his honey one and tilts his head at me in question.

"Toby, can you, uh, help me with something inside?" I grab his elbow and steer him toward the house, ignoring the stares of Pete and Jack behind us. Who cares what they think I need help with? I've put up with them loving on each other for literally years. They can deal.

"What is it?" Toby asks, depositing his empty champagne flute on a table as I propel him through the French doors into the kitchen. The large space is overrun with catering crew who pay us no attention.

"I need—you," I say, honest and raw.

He nods, as if he understands, then glances around. "Um—where?"

I think about the best place, decide on an upstairs bathroom, and drag him up the stairs. "I need this." I find the guest bathroom and lock the door behind us.

"I did sort of leave you hanging this morning," Toby admits.

"You did that. But that's not it—I want you all the time."

"Good," is all he says, and then we're kissing, and fumbling with our flies, and then he's on his knees for me. The boy has been a fast study where blow jobs are concerned, and it's not long before he's drawing an orgasm out of me, longer and deeper and more unsettlingly good than a quick and dirty bathroom blow job should be. He swallows, and when he stands up and we kiss, I can taste myself on him.

"God, I love you."

"Kingston, love you, need you," he says, sounding wrecked. I'm the only one who's gotten off here, but I eye the floor dubiously—I'm not ruining my suit pants if I can help it.

"Hang on." I arrange a clean plush bath towel on the closed toilet lid and sit. My mouth is now the perfect height for Toby to feed me his cock, which he does enthusiastically.

"Oh fuck, yes, that's good," he says, pumping into me. "I need this. I need you. God, I need you Kingston, feels so good."

The breathless dirty talk makes me wish I could get it up again, but there's time for that later. I pull him close with my hands on his ass, and then Toby shouts and comes. I spit in the sink; we wash our hands, button our flies. Toby runs some water through his hair to make it more purposefully tousled than sex tousled, and I pat my beard with water.

"Do we look like we just had sex in a bathroom?" Toby asks as we emerge into the thankfully empty hall.

"We look like we're in love," I answer. He grins at me, and we hold hands as we return to the party, to our friends, radiating love, which is perfectly appropriate on this day of all days.

I know intellectually that this honeymoon period where we can't keep our hands off each other will fade into something more routine. That he'll get caught up in work and I'll need to travel and there will be days, maybe weeks, where we don't have sex. That'll be okay, as long as I can hear his voice in my ear, see his face over breakfast, have him next to me while I fall asleep. Everything and anything will be okay as long as we're together.

He's my must-have.

And I'm his.

EPILOGUE
KINGSTON

One year later

"HOLD STILL."

"I am holding still."

"Hold more still."

"I'm hungry. And horny."

"Five more minutes."

"That's a literal eternity."

"I'll make it worth your while."

I take a slow, deep breath, hold it for five, and let it out again just as slowly. It's a trick Toby taught me to deal with the boredom of live modeling. Sure, he could take photos, but I'm paranoid about creating digital evidence of me in my current state. So he's got an easel set up in the living room with a large piece of drawing paper on a board. I'm naked, and hard, per his request. He had this idea ages ago, but between my work schedule, his recent London art show, celebrating our friends as they experienced anniversaries and other milestone life events, it's been a busy year.

"Are you done?" I ask. My ass is numb.

"Five minutes isn't up yet."

"Seriously?"

"Almost."

I bite my lip and keep my cool. You'd think it would be hard to keep my erection for thirty minutes straight, but Toby had a fix for that. You see, I might be cock-out on the green velvet chair, but Toby's equally nude behind his easel. I can see everything, daydream about everything we love doing with each other. And since I've been in the city for the past three days, I have plenty of pent-up sexual frustration to work out on my boyfriend the second he puts the pencil down and tells me I can move.

"What are we doing for dinner?" I ask.

"Jack and Pete invited us over," he says absently, attention on his work in progress. "I told them we'd bring the wine."

"What are we having?"

"Not sure. But Jack said Beck's in charge of dessert."

My stomach lets out an audible rumble.

Toby snort-laughs. "You are hungry, aren't you?"

"I told you."

I watch my boyfriend erase something on his pad, then sketch again. He's beautiful when he works. He's beautiful all the time—but it's a privilege to see him like this, lost in his process, even if I'm doing my damnedest to distract him. He looks over the top of the easel at me, then makes another mark.

"Tobias Eric Wheaton, I know five minutes were up long ago," I say sternly.

"Fine—I'm done." He drops his pencil, wipes his hands on a nearby rag.

Finally. I shift in my seat, trying to restart my circulation. He walks two feet toward me, but I stop him with a growl.

"What—you're not even going to show me?"

Toby laughs. "I thought you were so ready for food and other things."

"Honey, please." I'm never above begging when it comes to him.

He retraces his steps, turns the easel toward me. It's a large drawing, simply me on the chair in the corner of the room, rendered in a detailed and incredibly realistic style.

"That's how you drew me?" I ask, aghast. In the drawing my eyes are heavy-lidded, my mouth parted, my body a collection of sinewy curves that's both an invitation and a promise.

Toby bites his lip, amused, and maybe a little nervous. He nods.

"I look..."

"Hot as sin," he says, finally crossing the room and straddling my lap. His skin is cold, and I wrap my arms around him to warm him up.

"Debauched," I counter.

"Decadent," he suggests.

"Depraved," I can't resist adding.

"You look amazing, Kingston. And since this picture is just for me, I made you just as wicked as I wanted to."

"Just for you, huh?"

"For my own personal pleasure," he says, kissing me soundly on the lips.

My hands drop to his bare ass and squeeze. He brushes his mostly soft dick against my mostly hard one and shivers. All thoughts of hunger, of boredom, of scandalous drawings done by my mischievous artist boyfriend fall away as I embrace him, lick into his mouth, and feel him grow aroused in my arms.

"I want to give you pleasure," I whisper.

He groans, rocking into me. "I love you so much, Kingston," he says, the simple statement sending an electric shock of need through me.

"Love you, honey," I say back, never taking the fact that he loves me and I love him for granted.

He lifts himself up, grasping my cock and positioning the tip at his entrance. At the immediate give of his body, I groan. "You minx," I say as he slides down, taking me effortlessly.

"I told you I'd make it worth your while," he says, a bit breathlessly, but the pride is there, too. He must have spent time prepping while I was driving up from the city.

I shift in the chair until we find an angle and a rhythm that makes me see stars and makes him plunge his tongue into my mouth. I kiss away his cries, overcome with the way his body's open for me, greedy for me.

"That feel good, honey?" I ask. I'm getting close.

In answer, he throws his neck back, bouncing up and down, his hand stripping his cock furiously. He shoots all over my stomach and chest, painting me with his come. He's spent, but he keeps up the rhythm like a champ until I let myself go, pouring my love into him, whispering it again over and over.

Eventually, we stop moving, stop telling each other

how good we feel, how much we love each other. We're on the green velvet chair, still joined, the wonderful mess growing cool on my belly. I look into Toby's amber eyes and he looks into mine. "Time to get ready for dinner," I say.

His pink mouth curves up. "You want to pick out what I'm going to wear?"

"Always. You want to pick out the wine?"

"Sure."

I'm not complaining about the scorching sex, but it's the little things like figuring out evening plans with the man I'm going to grow old with that make me truly happy.

A surprisingly loud meow comes from the direction of the kitchen.

We smile at each other. Then we get up to feed Luna together.

Thank you for reading the final installment in the Rosedale Seasons series! I hope you had a chance to read the summer, autumn, and winter books, plus Jack and Pete's story as told in *His Coffee Shop Crush*.

As a bonus, I'm sharing Beck's sugar cookie recipe, which is truly a foolproof classic.

Enjoy!

xoxo,

Elle

BECK'S CLASSIC SUGAR COOKIES RECIPE

ADAPTED FROM JUDY ROSENBERG

Ingredients:

2 ¼ cups all-purpose flour

½ cup granulated sugar

½ cup powdered sugar

1/8 teaspoon baking soda

1/8 teaspoon cream of tartar

½ teaspoon salt

12 ½ tablespoons unsalted butter, cold, cut into small pieces

1 large egg

1 tablespoon vanilla extract

Instructions:

Process dry ingredients in a food processor for 5 seconds. Distribute butter over the flour mixture and process for about 30 seconds until you get a coarse meal. Stir egg and vanilla together and pour through feed tube while processor is running. Process until dough comes together, 30 more seconds.

Remove dough to a work surface, knead to make it come together, then shape into a disk. Place disk between two large pieces of parchment paper, then roll out to 1/8-1/4 inch thickness depending on preference. Chill rolled dough in fridge or freezer. If it's going to be days before you bake, wrap parchment slabs in plastic wrap as well.

When ready to bake, preheat oven to 375 °F. Peel off both pieces of parchment paper. Use cookie cutters to cut shapes. Re-roll scraps as needed between parchment paper —chill in freezer for a few minutes between rolls if dough becomes too warm to work with. Bake on parchment paper covered cookie sheets for 10-15 minutes depending on size of cut cookies until lightly browned on edges. Cool on baking sheets. Ice and decorate as desired. Store in an airtight container. Enjoy!

ACKNOWLEDGMENTS

I can't quite believe we've come to the end of the seasons with *A Small Town Spring*. It was a joy to write through summer, autumn, winter, and spring. I'm really going to miss Kingston and the entire Rosedale crew...maybe they'll show up again down the line!

A million thanks to those people whose time and energy made this book better. Amanda Boes, you've been a champion of the series from the start and I thank you for your enthusiasm and support. For the amazing editing I thank Sara Kettler and Tracy of Amaze Inn Proofreading. Any mistakes are mine.

To my plot group and writer friends—thanks for keeping me going in the right direction. Dar of Wicked Smart Designs found the perfect Kingston for the cover. Thanks to Taylor Delong for the title.

Thank you so much to the readers who have loved this series. I write these books to be enjoyed, and it warms my heart every day knowing someone out there is reading these stories and smiling.

Here's to a happy, warm spring and to the magic that books bring us year-round.

xoxo,

Elle

ABOUT THE AUTHOR

Fueled by chocolate and canned wine, Elle Waters writes steamy, feel-good, small town romance with guaranteed happy endings. She lives with her family in Connecticut. Sign up for her newsletter to hear about her next release!

Elle loves to hear from readers at elle@ellewatersauthor.com.